WITHDRAWN
UTSA LIBRARIES

Lent: The Slow Fast

The Iowa Short Fiction Award

Prize money for the award is provided by

a grant from the Iowa Arts Council

Lent: The Slow Fast

STARKEY FLYTHE, JR.

UNIVERSITY OF IOWA PRESS

IOWA CITY

University of Iowa Press, Iowa City 52242
Copyright © 1990 by Starkey Flythe, Jr.
All rights reserved
Printed in the United States of America
First edition, 1990

No part of this book may be reproduced or utilized in any form or by any means, electronic or mechanical, including photocopying and recording, without permission in writing from the publisher. This is a work of fiction. Any resemblance to actual events or persons is entirely coincidental.

Some of these stories have previously appeared, in a slightly altered form, in the *South Carolina Review, Kansas Quarterly Review, Southwest Review, Ploughshares, Northwest Review, Antioch Review, Epoch, Permafrost, Best American Short Stories,* and *O. Henry Prize Stories.* The author is grateful to the Aiken County and South Carolina arts commissions and the National Endowment for the Arts for their kind and generous support.

The publication of this book is supported by a grant from the National Endowment for the Arts in Washington, D.C., a federal agency.

Printed on acid-free paper

Library of Congress Cataloging-in-Publication Data
Flythe, Starkey.
Lent: the slow fast/Starkey Flythe, Jr.—1st ed.
p. cm.—ᵛ(Iowa short fiction award)
Some of these stories previously appeared, in a slightly altered
form, in the South Carolina Review, and others.
Contents: Lent: the slow fast—The ice fisher—For a good time
call Matthew—CV10—The coalition—Every known diversion—
Learning Italian—Walking, walking—The water cure—The glass
of milk—Point of conversion.
ISBN 0-87745-274-1 (alk. paper)
I. Title. II. Series.
PS3556.L97L4   1990   89-29989
813'.54—dc20   CIP

**Library
University of Texas
at San Antonio**

For J. deW. F.

Contents

Lent: The Slow Fast

The phone rang Easter morning. Ten o'clock. Jo Ellen was lying in bed beside Chris. The children, old enough not to believe in the Easter bunny and young enough to be oblivious to the spurious relationship between chocolate and pimples, had grabbed their baskets and run off across the front yard to a neighbor's where she imagined they were analyzing the smears on each other's faces.

She had reached toward Chris, stretched really, found him halfway. The bedroom door was locked, the door the children banged on to wake her and Chris every morning. Years, she thought, since they'd had time for morning love. "One more privilege," she heard Chris say, "the middle class is being deprived of."

Jo Ellen found the phone across Chris's bare chest.

"I think there's been a breakdown in communications," Peter said. Peter was the priest at St. Xavier's. At the beginning of Lent, forty days before, he had weighed 230 pounds.

"A breakdown in communications?" she said, staring at Chris's erection under the blankets.

"Yes," Peter said. "You were supposed to fix breakfast for us—for the choir—this morning."

Jo Ellen thought she could hear Peter's hunger, heavy and boundless, shifting inside his vestments. She knew what must have happened. He had been late, rushing to eight o'clock mass—the nuns, their mass already celebrated, had called to him, "Father Peter, have some breakfast?" and he had replied, "No. Haven't got time," thinking all the while he'd get one of Jo Ellen's wonderful breakfasts, sausages she'd stuffed into the casings herself, the fluffy eggs scrambled with cheese, homemade muffins.

At the beginning of Lent, Ash Wednesday's cross barely washed off the congregation's forehead, Peter had bubbled from the pulpit—his text, "Feed My Sheep"—that St. Xavier's was going to "compensate for the inner city's unemployment with a Saturday soup kitchen."

"St. Xavier's," he'd said, "has the best cooks in the world and Jo Ellen Rostineau's the best of the best; we're making her head of the project!"

She and Chris were new in the city. People hadn't been very friendly to them until she began to cook. Now most of the people they knew and went out with, the children's friends, too, were people they had met at church, a benefit—"besides the guilt," Chris said—of being Catholic.

It was an easy step from feeding the sheep to feeding the shepherd. The first Saturday Peter had, simply in the line of pastoral encouragement, lifted the lid of one of her pots where she was cooking fresh pea soup and taken a whiff so deep and satisfying she thought the bells in the tower would clang. "Ahhh," he'd breathed, and what could she say but, "Try some"?

"Feed Cambodia?" Chris had told her two weeks later, foreign mission Sunday. "Why all the Christian Children's Fund has to do is slice the white meat from Peter's thighs: stuff Bangladesh."

Then Peter had asked her, again from the raised stage of the chancel, the cross behind him in authoritative support, to oversee a breakfast in the parish hall, "to bring everybody together during this special time. Maybe lead off with eggs Benedict?"

The third Sunday in Lent, eight A.M. service, he'd said in his homily, "I can smell delicious scents wafting in from the kitchen. No telling what all Jo Ellen isn't stirring up for us." It was so folksy—$2.00 apiece—attendance increased, and at Matins, too, as people could come for breakfast, get the children in Sunday School, and be in their pews by 10:30. Jo Ellen could hardly stand it, people knowing her name, asking her for recipes, hugging her: Peter asked her to put on a lunch, Wednesday. Then a dinner Thursday. It seemed she was at church every day. Businessmen's Bible class, Youth for Christ.

She had watched in astonishment as Peter, 230, became Peter, 250. His legs rubbed together when he walked, made a noise like taffeta skirts.

As Lent moved forward, Peter's sermons dealt increasingly with Bible feasts: the Wedding Feast at Cana, the Supper at Emmaus.

> The loaves and fishes [he intoned from the pulpit]: you can almost taste those crusty loaves, the insides light and airy, but chewy, and the fishes, those wonderful Mediterranean catches, skates and scampi, barely simmered in a little olive oil, a squirt of lemon, very simply prepared—all the Jewish culinary genius brought to bear on the boy's lunch.

Jo Ellen, aproned, sitting in the back poised to rush out at the benediction to push the fish under the broiler for lunch, could almost see the herbed oil dripping down Peter's lips.

> How thrilled that little boy must've been. Allowed to go off on his own, secure in the love of his mom who'd packed his lunch, wide open to faith, the scent of the fresh-baked bread and the marinated fish reaching his nostrils as he walked along the early morning way. Maybe a piece of goat cheese—feta or chèvre.

He looked right at Jo Ellen, going over the rows of parishioners whose Sundays (and Wednesdays and Thursdays) had been so pleasantly altered by her cooking. She tingled with pride.

> And how full of charity when the time came, how ready to be loving when HE asked this vast crowd if anybody there had food? How proud the boy was to say, "Here, Master, here am I. Take this, take all of this."

Jo Ellen stirred. The congregation had murmured somewhere between expectation and embarrassment, turning obliquely to each other as if a stranger who was not a member of the church and was never likely to be had come in the back door.

"What does he want?" Chris demanded, breaking her recollection, his hand flat against the inside of her leg, their bed warm with desire. His long fingers rested a minute before insisting. She propped her elbow on his chest. The plastic phone receiver was smooth as his skin. "Hang up!" Chris said.

"Peter? I talked with the organist. She said they sang better on an empty stomach. I put out some fruit, some cheese yesterday for them."

"Some cheese?"

"In the refrigerator." She knew he was calling from the church kitchen. The phone was right next to the refrigerator. Jo Ellen thought she heard him opening the door. The image was so strong she imagined his opening the door to their bedroom, mischievous, like the children, seeing her and Chris, advancing toward them, not sternly, but lovingly, pulling back the sheet and criticizing their lovemaking the way he would her vegetable soup.

"Well, we're all down here and there's nothing to eat," Peter said, speaking absently into the refrigerator. She heard his echoing voice strained through the cool racks, a voice hopeless and forlorn among wilted lettuce leaves, food they would never eat but could not bear to throw away.

"Don't you see the cheese?"

No answer. Paper rattled. She couldn't, she told herself, hear teeth sinking into white fontina any more than Peter could see her and Chris is bed, Chris's long smooth arms pulling her to him, his long smooth body hairless and pure in a way she thought only women's bodies could be. Only the ravenousness of the two men made any sound.

She heard the phone receiver—black like Peter's robe, slipping on its short cord from the church kitchen's Formica countertop, falling, dangling, *knock nothing, knock nothing.*

Jo Ellen felt she was falling, too, not just into the arms of a perfectly legitimate husband—the church had sanctioned that, at least, though you weren't supposed to do it just for fun—but into a mortal neglect of duty, the guilt she had felt the last few weeks of Lent because she had stopped putting on the meals when Peter had gone into the hospital about his weight.

She had felt so happy the first weeks of Lent; then one Saturday morning she'd had her feelings hurt. In the soup kitchen she had put out what she thought was a tasty meal: French toast, homemade quince jam, stewed apricots, ham. A little black child wrinkled his nose, looked down at his plate and up at his mother. "Oh, go on and eat it," she said. "I'll buy us something *good* later on." Peter was standing next to Jo Ellen. He put his arm around her. "You know you cross the most intimate boundaries when you offer food to people? Hey!"

She saw suddenly it was unreasonable: her spending more time at church cooking for strangers, or for God, than for Chris and the children at home. God—his brides, the nuns' meals witnessed—didn't care: canned peas, instant mashed potatoes, meat boiled to death.

Tim, Jo Ellen and Chris's son, had begun to fail math; their little girl, Kate, protesting being alone so much, had kicked in a glass bookcase door in her classroom.

Time. The house, the yard, the children. Chris's tie for tomorrow evaporated into her presence in the church kitchen. So easy saying yes, so hard doing, buying food, cooking it.

Chris had finally put his foot down. "I don't think I want to go anymore." Two weeks before Palm Sunday.

Jo Ellen's mouth opened and her mother, twenty years before, flew out. "But it's your obligation, your *sacred* obligation." Chris looked at her coolly, as if somewhere along the climb of their marriage, he'd made a mistake, left a piton out or a rope unknotted.

She'd taken refuge as she always had, in church, on her

knees, alone. She saw the congregation—the "audience," Chris called it—was thin. It was the weekend of the regionals, the basketball tournaments. Chris hadn't let little Tim go because of his math grades. Kate was being punished for the bookcase door.

Lost in thought, Jo Ellen hadn't heard for a minute the assistant priest praying for Peter. Peter was in the hospital, he said. Diverticulosis. The assistant priest, a stickler for detail, said they were feeding him nothing but Jello. Raspberry Jello. She could see it in the stained glass window over the alter, the color of clear, translucent blood.

The news that Peter was sick had calmed her, equalizing her guilt over not wanting to cook for the church anymore and her anger with Chris.

Kneeling, she had imagined buckets of Jello in the hospital corridors. The light poured in through the stained glass window, and with the light, a sense of loss. In the dazzling light she saw the white communion dress of her childhood consumed. She had tempted Peter. His being out of control was her fault. Her melted butter, her heavy cream, had forced his vascular walls. Her wrongs transcended the church's.

The last time she'd seen Peter, he'd seemed huge but fine. She'd been in the kitchen, bent over the oven, drawing a skewer from a line of lamb kabobs. The air was sweet with onions and bell peppers bubbling in butter. She hadn't known he was behind her. Burning her fingers slightly, she had lost her balance and tumbled backward across the kitchen, shoving Peter in her path. The thought of impaling him on the skewer had crossed her mind. Stuck, the air would have hissed out of him slowly.

Everybody, she thought, had suffered from her talents. Her children. Chris. The garden, which should've been plowed, ready for the seed Good Friday when they always planted, was a tangle of last summer's weeds.

She knelt long after the assistant priest had absolved them. When she opened her eyes, everyone was gone. Snakes of smoke rose from the extinguished candles. She felt a part of her, a noisome duty, had been extinguished, too. The altar guild woman was stripping the flowers from either side of the cross and the last note of organ music hung in the air, an accusation.

The assistant priest was waiting at the back of the church. She shook his hand. He was tall and thin with a beard. He looked ascetic but someone had told her he had his own stockbroker.

"Aren't you going to feed us?" he asked.

"I didn't think anybody was coming. The basketball."

"Weren't you going to feed Peter?"

"I didn't know he'd gone into the hospital. I feel so sorry. There should be something. I always have something."

He followed her through the church, the robing room, to the kitchen. He sat down at the table, his expression and posture a history of husbands waiting for wives to feed them. She put down a paper-towel mat in front of him.

"Coffee?"

"I have to go to the hospital," he said. "The chaplains have a pool. I won't get home till after eleven."

She saw them, in black bathing suits, racing each other in the blue chlorine water. She put the plate down, the cup and saucer, the knife, spoon, and fork, though she had only a chicken sandwich and potato salad for him.

She watched him bite into the sandwich. Was she laying the same curse on him she'd put on Peter? The bite left a jagged half moon on the bread, the shape of a cry.

He sighed as if he wanted to take Peter's place in her ministrations. "You don't know how good this is!"

"I made the mayonnaise," she said, looking at the tiny white dots of it on his moustache and lips. He licked at the spots.

She put potato salad on his plate. He ate it with the exhilaration Peter had shown when he spoke of roasting the fatted calf for the prodigal son.

"More?"

He put his plate up, a mendicant.

She plopped one big spoonful on the plate. He held it there, still. She put another half chicken sandwich on it. He steadied the plate. She scraped the bowl.

She watched him eat, seeing Peter blowing up in this man's thin face. He put his plate up to her again and cocked his head a little, waiting.

Resolved, she had gone home then, surfacing among her housework, a diver with the bends, overcome by the enormity of small tasks. At first, the work, unpraised by Peter or the other parishioners, unsanctioned by God, had seemed sacrilege. Then, digging in the vegetable patch, dust-mopping under her and Chris's bed, making school lunches, became quietly satisfying.

Peter called when he got out of the hospital. She had left food in the church kitchen freezer. He wanted her to come thaw it. He cornered her when she went in Palm Sunday, saying, "You're still the chairman of the committee." He said "still" as if the appointment was eternal. He had lost very little weight though she had heard the doctors had taken out his entire lower tract and cleaned it on a towel. She felt an odd love for him as a person. "If the people aren't here," he said, speaking to a child, "we can't very well ask Him to be here." She listened for the capital "H" as if it were coming from a long way off. She thought of the hugs of ten anonymous women in the church kitchen, of how their embraces had been worth so much more than little Kate's defiance or Tim's math grades. Public love. Could she ever go back to the small arms of the children, Chris's alembic grasp?

As Chris soothed her now, Easter, in his arms, sun pouring through their bedroom window, little bubbles of pleasure popping through her body, she remembered trying unsuccessfully to calm Peter, unable to use physical means as Chris could with her.

She closed her eyes. This seemed right, this feeling, the results—children—the church and life for once coinciding. Chris's weight, usually gentle upon her, bore down. She closed her eyes tighter. She imagined someone dancing on his back. Peter? The weight seemed to increase. The weight, heavier and heavier, tried to exorcise the exquisite pleasure she felt. She wondered if she'd hung up the phone, whether she could. Whether her connection with Peter could be severed. The weight bore down, heavier and heavier. Dozing, the pleasure seemed farther and farther away. When she opened her eyes, the bed was shaking. Little Kate was jumping up and down. Tim was behind her shaking the headboard. Chris, a sheet draped loosely around his waist, leaned on the windowsill, looking at her, waiting. She thought he might have been St. Sebastian waiting for his arrows. The hole in her stomach where breakfast should've been whimpered, harmonizing in her mind with the other stomachs she'd left empty at the church. Everyone must suffer: that was Lent. She saw the eggs in the children's baskets. There was a new one: chocolate with a yellow fondant yolk. She wanted one. The thought of taking it from them, against their will, gave her an odd pleasure.

The Ice Fisher

Denny Harrell presses against the school wall trying to keep his underwear pants from falling down. He grips the elastic waistband, which has failed after service to five older brothers, in his fist hard enough to choke off the circulation in the bottom half of his body. Except for his being alone while the other children are playing, the pose appears fairly natural. His face is red, though. His eyes sting from not crying.

When the bell rings ending recess, while pretending to scratch his back Denny creeps to the rear of the line filing into the cafetorium. He thinks of it as a crematorium. He will be burned alive on the low stage when he sings, "I Dream of Jeanie with the Light Brown Hair." The underwear, made of hateful wool of a quality to last forever, will fall below his short pants. He will have to let the waistband loose when he gestures, as Mrs. Hutson, his fifth-grade teacher and the music mistress of the school, has instructed. He imagines he can drown the titters and snickers of the other students with his singing. Actually his voice is clear and strong, without a waver. He likes to sing. He looks straight at his audience and opens his mouth wide. He sneaks his breaths skillfully, has huge lungs for nine. His torso looks like a barrel with toothpicks for legs.

The teacher in charge of getting the children to their seats suddenly stares at him. Denny puts his hands up to his mouth in the pre-vomit sign, eyes wide, cheeks puffed out, hand to mouth. She calls, "Harrell! Denny Harrell! Where are you going? Get back in this line!"

But Denny is in the boys' basement, pulling down his short pants. He takes off his shirt. The underwear is in one piece, an arrangement, he thinks, of almost historical significance. He tears open the buttons of the underwear, heavy as a wet blanket, protection and elasticity dead after six hating owners. He is surprised at his violence, but wads the underwear suit into a sodden ball and throws it over the booth hoping for a direct hit. He is not good at sports. There is a satisfying ploop. His father, whose favorite sport is ice fishing, will come back with

15

him and make him retrieve the garment. The thought of fishing through the toilet for the vile underwear curdles his stomach. Only then the bathroom will be full. The boys in his class who never choose him for teams will point and whistle and laugh and his father will be on their side. When his father takes him ice fishing on weekends and he endures the misery of sitting on a bucket in a tiny shack filled with cigar smoke, his father always asks Denny, "Did they pick you this time?"

Denny sees himself in the broken mirror over the sink, his tiny penis like a nib on some machine, on a sink disposal, to stop it running or get it started after it has chewed up a spoon.

He puts on his clothes; he looks five pounds thinner as he rushes to his place by the stage. Mrs. Hutson beams at him, relieved.

After a nursery-rhyme act in which a first-grader jumps over a lighted candle, nimbly, while the fire marshal looks on, Denny comes onstage; Mrs. Hutson strikes the piano. The notes reek of meals past, giving the tune a pizza flatness. Denny's voice is full of force, out of all proportion to his undernourished appearance; the audience, squirmy on the uncomfortable benches, is silent. The music pours over them with a calm that defeats the planned derision of the older boys.

Denny's confidence is free of malice or competition, joyfully technical. When he sings, "I dream," the listeners think of the power of dreams to make wishes come true, to prophesy, to rest them, to create an escape, and they are quiet.

The older boys never choose him, but each is aware he can sing and anyone who can do something is important: fart in class so the teacher can't see; play catcher close enough to the plate to make overhead-pops outs.

The clapping is spontaneous. It roars from the back, runs down the side aisles, surprises Denny. He stands, face open to the crowd, happy, unconsciously milking the applause until boys in the back are whistling and banging on the benches. Mrs. Hutson holds up her finger for silence but she is drowned.

Finally she says, "Please, please. Perhaps Denny will oblige us with another number? Would you like that?" Denny senses the response is to a game, an answer to the folly of Mrs. Hutson's putting a question to the pit, the knowledge classes will be delayed. There is pleasure, though, in his being the cause of pleasure.

Mrs. Hutson whispers him off the stage to the piano. They agree on "Tenting Tonight." She has not had time to instruct him in the elocution, in the inane gestures of grade-school performance. She has to make up for it by explaining the words.

"Brother has been fighting brother in this terrible war," she says. "Both sides are losing. They are hungry and tired. Many are wounded and sick, far from loved ones. Before the soldiers lie down on the cold ground, they sing this song."

Someone moans "Boohoo," but the mockery is short-lived. Denny stands very straight, his voice pours out, pure and full. Without Mrs. Hutson's gestures, the effect of the song is simple and sad. He draws the words through the tune a little behind the tempo (she must speak to him about that) until it is almost a lullaby and the students, tired from recess, stare, wide-eyed, frozen in the moment before sleep. When he finishes, the words die into a long fall of quiet. The children are more asleep than awake, metamorphosed somehow into the gray and blue soldiers around the campfire.

Mrs. Hutson lets herself cry behind her glasses, thinking of the South, her background the only superiority, romantic superiority, she has over the other teachers. She imagines the salted and burned fields, the disenfranchised men, Jeff Davis in chains. Her grandfather was from New Jersey, though. The moment is long. Some students are thinking of tests next period, hoping they will be put off. Another teacher has a different picture of Denny, always against the school yard wall, his hands behind him. A visitor, Dr. Sydenstricker, in the audience, an annual visitor at the request of the school district music teachers' association, thinks what a beautiful voice.

Billy Sydenstricker is the choir master at the Cathedral of St. Mary the Virgin. The choir operates a school next to the cathedral, a day school. The choir is heavily endowed. Billy goes to every school in the district looking for boy sopranos. Usually, if they have the voice, he can't purify their diction, *Cheeses* for *Jeezus*. Or they are shy and hide behind the choir screen. There are four places behind the choir screen at the foot of each row. They are all taken and there is a waiting list. Or they bring discipline problems.

"It's a great opportunity for him," Denny's mother, Rayanne, tells her husband, Hugo.

"I don't want my son growing up to be no mackerel snapper!" he says.

"You don't have to convert, the brochure says," Rayanne tells him, not quite convinced herself. "It would cost us six thousand dollars a year to send him there."

"It would cost us ten thousand dollars to send him to the moon, but we ain't going to."

"He'd learn a lot about music. They take these nice trips in summer. Go to Rome, Italy, and France. Europe."

"I want him to stay here with me. I want to take him ice fishing. I want the boys to choose him!"

"Who's better to choose? Some kids who don't like him anyway, or a school where he'll have teachers interested in him? You never get that, do you, that some people just don't like you and they're never going to choose you? He might get into rock and roll. They make a good living. They get rich!"

"No, not going, that's that!"

The following Monday, Rayanne takes Denny, dressed in another pair of hand-me-down wool underwear, a talisman to protect him against her disobedience, to the cathedral school.

The brothers smile condescendingly at her and Denny as if they comprise the whole of Protestant literature and art, its temporariness in the face of Giotto and Dante and Michelangelo.

The nuns, out of the mystery of their veils and long dresses now, try to out-ordinary the ordinariness of Protestantism.

But Dr. Sydenstricker takes them into the cathedral. From the concrete block of the church she and Hugo sometimes go to, this soaring miracle is a solace of myth and sorrow and triumph.

In the church—ribbed like the inside of the whale that spit out Jonah, she hears from the very back pew Denny's voice, white and high like a beam of light caught in the vault, a voice to make her unafraid of Hugo, or guiltless of her own wrong-doing. He sings hymns—she can't think they are Catholic songs, maybe the choir master has a book from their church to make Denny feel at home—and she feels for moments like the Virgin Mary herself, brimming with observations she must keep in her heart. Would Joseph have struck Mary, though?

"You took him where?" Hugo demands at supper. He already knows—his bus went right by the cathedral and, luck being luck, there they were emerging.

"If I told you not to and that was that and you still went on and did it, you must have a very good reason, probably better than my reason for not letting him go, that I don't want him to be a sissy and I don't want fried fish stinking up the house on Fridays, right? I forgive you. And just in case," and he comes across her mouth with the side of his right hand, hard, clean—she thinks of it as Denny's voice, on key, perfect pitch—how can Hugo be so deadly accurate?—an inch one way or the other would've saved her. A random inch.

Her jaw is so sore she cannot open her mouth to eat. She needs to lose weight, she tells herself. Hugo apologizes. "How could I?" he demands. His eyes menace. She thinks he will hit her again if she doesn't answer.

Five sons, plus Denny. The youngest lying about his age like his brothers to get into the Marines. Sending an allotment home. Hugo supported the armed services—"the happiest days of my life," he said whenever Rayanne thought he should say he was happy with her. "I want all my brats in it. Denny included. He don't show no signs of wanting to join. It's time he should be asking about it." Like his remark they could send Denny to the moon or China. She risked being hit to say, "Well, neither do I," and he hit her.

She was raised in a family where to be male was to be violent. Her mother never reprimanded her father for letting go about things, chided him for not. She felt more secure knowing his fist could protect her, anywhere she walked in the neighborhood, than she would have knowing his paycheck never deviated as it always did, between factory and home.

But Hugo's not being able to see any difference in people—perhaps it is like acceptance of his hand across her face, a male prerogative—makes her nervous and, after making her nervous, makes her determined. Denny is going to that school and will open his mouth in the procession.

The first Sunday he is to be in the choir, scrubbed white as a piece of tallow, Hugo is called in to work overtime. Rayanne thanks God and tries to cross herself, imagining she is hitting all the wrong places.

She puts on a hat she hasn't worn in years, forces her too-fat fingers into short gloves, and lopes for the bus. Denny has been picked up hours earlier by a van from the church. She sits in the back, astonished at the casual dress of people coming and going, paying very little attention to the priest at the altar. And then the children march in. The organ notes pound the stone floor. The descant rises above the general tune and the singing of the congregation the way an eagle would soar over sparrows. Even above that she hears Denny. He comes close to her pew in the procession.

A motet at the offering throws the voice back to her, to every ear in the congregation with the intensity of sun magnified by glass. He is hidden, so she cannot see him. But she knows his voice and she can imagine perfection.

Leaving the cathedral she wants to tell someone. But no one seems friendly. Stinging sleet drives her back into the vestibule to wait for Denny. They have a half-hour practice before he can leave. Rayanne is embarrassed by her hat, the shortie white gloves. People talk, but not to her. Nervous, she thinks words mean nothing. The priests could have cocked their fingers and everybody would have flocked to the altar; the man preaching the sermon might have shaken his head. No! Hugo hit her; she knows what that means. When the children open their mouths, music is more important than words. Music goes through the body, pulls strings, makes chords with what is already there. Only words go through the mind. The music hangs in her ears like water lilies in a pool, sweetening and filling the air. She feels Denny's voice is somehow the sex she has never understood or felt pleasure in with Hugo, satisfying and long, an act perfect if never repeated or if repeated a thousand times.

When he comes to her, his face is that of another child, holy, dazzling, beautiful. He cannot stop talking to her, telling her everything that happened, what they said to him. The priests complimented him. Singled him out. Dr. Sydenstricker wanted him to sing a solo at the end of the month. He marched in the procession with some boys who lived near. He could ride with them.

Hugo is waiting for them when they get home.

"What's for the old man's dinner?" he asks, furious. She has forgotten, or, having remembered, thought she would be home in time. She tears into the kitchen. Denny's bright face ravishes the sullenness of Hugo's overtime, his disappointment at not being able to go out to the lake and bore a hole.

Hugo has heard something. Over the unsatisfying lunch he tries to remember who told him, or if he told someone at the plant about Denny's boys' choir, or how the choir director found him. It is something about organists. Or choir masters. He drinks another beer to clear his memory.

During the week he sulks over Rayanne's getting Denny into the school, over Denny's enthusiasm, his new friends, the face that seems less and less like his own, and happier and happier to be so.

Sunday morning, Denny gone, he tells Rayanne he is going out to see if he can find somebody to go ice fishing with him. He looks funny, she thinks, his clothes vaguely like her hat and white gloves, but she lets it go, is determined to make up for last Sunday's dinner.

Hugo goes to the cathedral, walks up the center aisle to the front pew. He glances from side to side, tries to ape the genuflections and crossings of the people sitting around him, saying out loud as he touches his forehead and his chest, "Head, gut, tit, tit." No one pays any attention to him. He crosses and recrosses his legs: his dress boots with very high heels have sharp inner points, which cut into his thighs and bang his ankles when he stands or kneels. He cranes his neck to see Denny, tells an old woman in black sitting next to him, "My son!" She stares blankly. He says, "Sounds just like a girl!" She moves to another seat. Her hearing aid catches the gleam from the bank of candles with a money-box in the middle. He gets up in the middle of the creed, goes over and drops a coin in, blows out a candle, all the while trying to remember who told him.

When the priests hold the host up, he leaps from the pew and gallops to the altar. He looks right, left, to see what to do, holds the wine a long time to his lips, his heavy, hairy hands forcing the delicate white fingers of the priest tight on the foot of the chalice. He stands five minutes in the middle of the choir searching for Denny, finds him, and winks.

In his seat he stretches his arms over his head and yawns loudly, uncomfortable in being uncomfortable, miserable for having come. He wishes, kneeling, his legs too long, his frame too big for the narrow pews, that he had the same habit of faith as these people around him. During the endless prayers, said rapidly and to no one in particular, his eyes dart back and forth between Denny and Dr. Sydenstricker's arms, with slits in his surplice, waving the air when the children sing. His lips mouth the words, his eyebrows move up his forehead as if they were leaving his face altogether. At an amen, he touches a boy's head. Hugo stares at his hand on the shiny gold hair, the large ring on Sydenstricker's finger, the way the hand lingers. It begins to come back to him. Hugo turns red.

After the mass, he waits and waits for Denny. What has happened to him? Finally, Hugo strides back into the church and finds a door into the parish hall. The mood of the acolytes and priests, the women taking the flowers from the altar and locking up the silver, disturbs him. They are cheerful, as if they were cleaning up after a party.

"Where's the choir?" he demands of the crucifer who is polishing the brass cross.

The boy points to a flight of stairs. Hugo hears a piano, like the sound in a bar. He imagines Denny leaning in the bend of the instrument the way he saw a woman at a concert on television. He takes the steps three at a time.

There are two gothic doors at the top. He throws open the door on the right. The choir, still robed, is going over and over a phrase. Dr. Sydenstricker stops, looks at him with irritation. Denny is in front, standing, a sheet of music in his hands. Hugo plunges into the middle of the room, feels the humiliation of Sydenstricker's cold inquisitive stare.

"Touch him! I'll find out!" he shouts, realizes with each word he is saying that something is wrong. The silence puzzles him. He expects Sydenstricker to answer in kind, craves the simplicity of a fight. The boys, till now only mildly interested, used to interruptions on Sunday, mothers who have to take sons early, priests making suggestions about the music in the service, now turn their attention to Dr. Sydenstricker. Hugo feels in the false exuberance of their glance that they are allies. He swells bigger and bigger; his words seem to kill the music lingering in the room. The more he threatens, the more aware he is of some mistake, some cat of innocence let out of the bag. The boys now stare at him. Denny's face and mouth twist in pain. Hugo is reminded of Rayanne's face after he hit her; a dead silence blocks out his presence. The more he talks, the more the silence punishes him. He is moving back against the wall, out of the center. Denny is praying to his new god that

Hugo will not identify himself as his father. Hugo grabs the door handle. "You come downstairs, Denny!" He slams the door.

Denny wishes that Hugo was wilder. They could have understood a madman. But there was a vile reasonableness in what he said. The other boys look at Dr. Sydenstricker, who feels curiously sunk, unable to defend or explain himself. Idiot! He has never touched one of them.

He stands up by the piano, looks at Denny, and blows into his pitch pipe. They finish two glorias, neither prompted nor corrected by Sydenstricker. "That's all," he says and turns his back to them, standing at the keyboard, stacking music. He sees Denny, whose eyes are wet. He hates the tears, despises himself for bringing Denny into the fold. What has Denny told his father? What do the other children tell theirs?

Hugo is waiting for Denny. Denny lowers his head. Hugo puts his great hairy hand under his face and lifts it up. It is so different from his own face. Rayanne is always saying, "Why won't you leave him alone? He's different. He doesn't want to go ice fishing." Hugo looks at her in Denny's face and thinks of her, or himself thirty years from now when they will look so much alike strangers will think they are brother and sister. Isn't that what love is, his face demands of hers? Making somebody *like* you? He looks at Denny's face again. It is so different. Denny has put his hand up to take his father's fist away. He takes the hand dutifully and they cross the street. He wants to ask him what he is mad at Dr. Sydenstricker about, supposes it is the same thing he is mad at Rayanne and himself about. Denny has the feeling he is leading Hugo. He hopes they are not going ice fishing. If he catches a cold, he won't be able to sing. He thinks of the space between the water and the ice, of the trapped air, the fish with no way to escape but Hugo's bread-baited hook. He tries to pull his hand free from his father. His underwear pants, the one condition Rayanne exacts of him for going to the choir school, sag. She is waiting dinner on them but Hugo decides to go straight to the lake.

For a Good Time
Call Matthew

Matthew is twenty, twenty-one, weighs the same, Jeannie thinks, watching him stripped to the waist, mowing the neighborhood lawns. An exaggeration, of course, but she is struck by how little is sufficient, necessary in the human body. The rest, bulges and swellings, are anthropological advertising, hype, oversell. The body, like an insect, a pumpkin bug, a firefly, exudes a scent, casts a light, to attract not just a mate but a perfect stranger.

Twenty-six, a widow, a good deal less than pretty, hair unruly though skin good, Jeannie sits at her dining room table glad for the prepayment death clause on the house, sad she can't find more happiness in the perfect order of her dead husband's business affairs. One kiss from the living, she reflects, is worth all the balanced checkbooks in the world.

She misses him out of loneliness, but out of a sense of failed love, too, that marriage and children for him were only parts of business success and she could never make him see otherwise.

She hears her son, Olney, age two, also paid for, college, medical, dental, crying. She pushes away the papers waiting to be signed in the probate of William's will just as Matthew with an odd grace turns the corner of the row. The grass flies behind his machine. The scent of clover wafts through the open screen door.

She goes into the bedroom, picks up Olney, whose never-cut gold hair, baby skin, sleep-stained eyes fail to conceal his origins: son of an insurance agent. William's dwelling on eventualities, she thinks sometimes, a whole sackful of "God Forbids," almost made them happen.

"Marry a man who knows something about business," her mother cautioned. "Your father would have done better if he'd known something." He is still alive. He knows that much.

She puts Olney in his high chair in the kitchen. He resists his bib, screaming for the strawberry yogurt, gleefully painting his face, chest, similar parts of her body pink.

He seems to delight in using her as a mother as his father, William, used her as a beneficiary. What she wanted was less clear. She has been, is, useful to them, even loved by them. It is love and use, though, with a purpose, Olney's in growing up, William's in dying, that confuses her. In both she has to remain behind, a widow, a woman alone by the fire waiting for her son to call when the rates go down with the sun for the evening. William, from an even longer distance, will make his demands, too. Memory.

Olney slops more yogurt, saying in dumb show, You have to bathe me anyway.

She washed the kitchen windows twice in her early days of widowhood when she was determined to keep busy, to forget her in-laws' shabby treatment of her and Olney. William's parents, excused by geography (they lived in Oregon) and geriatrics (William was the youngest of seven children, born when his parents were in their forties), plus the blessing of numerous other grandchildren, left her conspicuously alone.

Jeannie sees Matthew raking over the grass. He has a grass catcher, doesn't like to use it. The light bamboo rake bounces over the new-mown grass.

The neighbors complain he isn't reliable. "I told him," Mrs. Canley said to Jeannie, "to come every week and mow whether it needed it or not."

The Canleys have some kind of grass that doesn't grow fast or seed itself or admit weeds. William was fascinated by it, was making plans to resod their lawn when he had the first attack. The grass would seem ideal, she thinks, but it doesn't blow in the wind or smell sweet in the sun. It lies there, thick and ruggy, last to green in spring, first to brown in fall. Still, it is an easy mow. "Why won't you?" Jeannie asked Matthew. He had a way of reaching down into his feet for his voice. She thought of it traveling up his long legs, the wiry thin torso, and finally out the bearded lips that also sing bluegrass. "Well, it isn't any fun," he said.

"Fun!" William howled. "Fun! Cutting grass fun!" When he died, Jeannie thought his notion of fun, his objection to it as what was wrong with this country, might've brought on the coronary.

She remembered going on a trip, the only vacation she and Olney and William had ever taken—generally he thought vacations were a waste of time and money despite her argument, backed up statistically, that employers didn't give employees vacations because they loved them, that they worked better when they came back. They were in the car, packed to the gills. Matthew, who was to mow the lawn and pick up the mail and change the lights around inside the house and who was holding a list composed by William long enough and complicated enough to whip inflation and cure the common cold, looked up and said when William started the car, "Don't forget the main thing!" The effect was astonishing. Matthew had never ventured anything like that. William turned off the engine. Jeannie thought for a minute William was going to argue about just what the main thing was. Matthew, eyes slightly defiant, said, "Have a *good* time!" He drawled the "Good" so it seemed to wrap around three syllables, said it again. "Have a gu-u—d time." William cranked the car with a kind of fury as if an ant held up a convoy of kings. He roared out of the driveway. Jeannie looked back—something William said never do—and saw Matthew in the dust of the road, like the old joke, turned sideways so he was almost invisible. From that moment William pushed away the daffodils one was supposed to sniff going through life. The daffodils were on top of the picnic basket. She was always tying a posy to his lunch box when he went on day trips. At the dinner table he always moved flowers aside, saying they might be poison, that they would get into the food, or that they were stepping stones to bring in insects.

The screen door rattles gently. She looks up and sees Matthew, his chest pinky tan, his paps spreading out in beautiful uselessness, waist small enough to pass through a wedding ring. Masculine, she thinks, yet blatantly sexless. He has never by a glance or a word suggested sex to her. It is not a conscious avoidance, simply an absence.

"You think I could have a glass of ice water?" he asks. Olney glistens. Matthew is the only person he really likes in the whole world. His father competed with him, both after some big insurance policy. Jeannie he tries.

He will never be a mama's boy. He will never be anybody's boy. He is his own. That he didn't get from her, she thinks, pulling ice trays out of the freezer. She depends on someone else, is not convinced independence is the be-all, end-all. Independence implies making somebody else dependent.

"Looks like a commie pinko," Matthew says to Olney. "You'll never get by a house un-American activities committee in that strawberry shirt." Olney goes wild, screaming to be picked up. "Wed!" he says. "That's Raid," Matthew says, dealing nonsensically with the color, picking Olney up. Olney lays his head against Matthew's bare neck in the most loving gesture, the snuggle he almost achieves when she reads to him from his picture books.

Matthew sits down at the kitchen table, Olney in his lap. "You know you ought to wear a bib," he says, touching the splattered yogurt. Olney screams, "Beebee!" Jeannie ties the Beebee around his fat little neck. Olney beams with pride. "Too little, too late," Matthew says. "Maybe it'll work next time," Jeannie says. "Thanks."

"Or you'll get a rubber sheet draped around you," Matthew threatens.

Matthew stands up, puts Olney, obedient for once, in his chair where he digs into his baby spinach and carrots, looking shyly up at Matthew for approval. Matthew denies it in a very different way from William. William spoke to Olney from a height, with a concentration that willed the child to grasp his commands. Matt, a high school graduate, or less, responds to Olney as a person whose amusement value is at least equal or better than that of adults around him.

FOR A GOOD TIME CALL MATTHEW

Jeannie notices Matthew's leg. He is wearing cut-off jeans and along the calf and across his knee and up the inside of his thigh is a cut with the ugly clotted X-ing of sutures on both sides.

"Matt! Your leg! What on earth?"

"Well, nothing much."

"Nothing much! You must have a hundred stitches!"

He turns red, noticing her looking at his leg.

"Wed!" Olney gurgles, wiggling his baby spoon.

"What?" she demands.

"Oh, we was riding out along highway 56. This semi came along. I didn't think they ever used that old back road, and another truck was coming the other way and he had to get over and they rather hit you than slow down."

"The truck *hit* you?"

"Well, *pushed* me."

"Were you alone?" Jeannie blushes at the question, like "Are you married?"

"Ed, you know, sometimes helps me cut grass, we were riding along on our bikes. Twenty-five miles out, not a care."

"It's a wonder you weren't killed."

"It's a wonder."

"What did they do?"

"Just edged us. I got caught on a guard rail and went along a spell. Ed got his bike mashed up."

"What did they do?"

Matthew puts his finger on his nose, crosses his eyes at Olney, and says, "Am I repeating myself?"

"I mean, what did they do to compensate?"

"Oh, took us to the emergency room. Bought Ed a new bike. Gave us some money. But heck, we was having a good time. They can't do nothing to make up for spoiling that."

"It's filthy," Jeannie says, "look at the grass stains! You've got oil and dirt in the cut. You better let me wash it. Here, just sit over here!"

"Got a extra Beebee? Buddy?" he says to Olney. Olney tries to take his off.

"Put your leg up," Jeannie says, coming back with the cotton and boric acid.

"This ain't for publication," he says to Olney.

It is his right leg. His basketball shoes are the old kind with globes of the world over each ankle. With his legs spread, one on the table, the other on the floor, she notices without really seeing that he is not wearing any underwear. He turns red. The idea of spontaneous combustion flashes in her mind. She remembers William's boxer shorts worn as a result of an article he read about increased male potency out of jockey shorts.

She touches the wound with the wet cotton. Grass stains the cotton green. Olney watches with intense concentration, his tiny brow wrinkled into a spiderweb. His presence reassures Jeannie of the innocence of the operation. Matthew's leg is as long as a dimension of the kitchen wall. She watches the skin goose pimple from the cool boric acid. She admires the power of the flesh to heal, to reduce someday the rickrack of the stitches to a thin white scar. She wonders why the heart is so unsteady, so violent in its desire to enshrine wounds, systematically cataloguing them for future resentments.

Her eyes, as if on stems, periscopes attached to her sexual longing and emptiness, stare as if from a great distance at Matthew's groin, thrilling, as she had as a girl, at the difference between men and women.

William initiated sexual contact with the question "What are you thinking?" which meant "Are you thinking the same thing as I am?" She would nod. To him it was a contract. Each party to agree. There must be a consideration. There was a missing wildness though, the stiff wind, the storm she tried to dismiss as romantic longing, the sweet discontent a woman wanted in her lover.

"Does that hurt?" she asks Matthew.

"No worse than poison ivy. All in the itch. Your grass going to need it today?"

Jeannie feels a flash of fire cross her neck, her cheek, the question is so close to William's "What are you thinking?"

"Come into the bathroom and let me rinse and dry that up," she says, blushing again at how her voice is reduced to the cycle of the washing machine; rinse, dry. William liked that in a woman, did not want her to work outside his home.

Matthew slides his leg off the table. Olney tries to imitate him in a gesture pure Gary Cooper.

The bathroom, the half bath, is under the stairs. The fixtures are narrowly designed, the hand basin is a half circle, the small toilet fits catty-cornered into the angle of the walls.

Matthew puts his leg up on the hand basin. Awkwardly, she tries to rinse the dirt from the rest of his leg without getting water on the wound. He stands, uneasily stork-like, his lack of protest another sign, she thinks, of innocence.

For a second he loses his balance. Jeannie, grasping for a full circle, forgets the basin is only half and stumbles against the wall. Their lips swipe each other like the back of a hand cleaning a mouth. A whiff of his bubble gum penetrates her brain. She becomes small, a responding insect. The half inch that separates their lips, the mile-wide space that separates their lives, closes down, the end of a trip, a familiar house, not quite home, in sight. He kisses her with the hard passion of a man fleeing boyhood, one kiss, handless, gropeless, a rock of sudden substance in the vacant landscape of her life. She returns the kiss, trying to reassure herself biology, not reason, is manipulating her. Not comfort a woman needs, she thinks, but being wanted, responded to, equally, fairly with the same faith William had in the business, in his partners, something more than transitory craving or the respectful duty he seemed to owe, like a mortgage, to his wife.

William would've had no faith in her being able to resist Matthew, could not have understood what was being resisted or what came out of resistance, the force of nature, the creator of self-strength, strength to be and not be afraid, to give in and not be obliterated by weakness, to come back, not losing self but knowing self did not exist if not given, even in error. Her will, second by second, builds, becomes a wall. Matthew stares at her with love or something equivalent in his eyes. Slowly she realizes it is his leg he is asking for. Falling, she clutched the leg so hard the circulation was cut off. As she lets go, the white calf slowly diffuses with blood, the thigh loses its crimson.

Letting go. She went to the wrong place to let go. Church. Parents without Partners. William loved the church, an enormous warehouse modeled after the baths of Diocletian. The interest on the building was $60,000 a month and the Sunday School classes were divided by professions, doctors, lawyers, professors, according to their ability to nurse the staggering debt. "Why do you go?" she asked William. He said, "Grandfather always told me better to be seen coming out of church Sunday morning than a pool hall! Besides, I might make some contacts!" Desperate, misguided, she went to PWP for fellowship, solace. Dancing with an overweight man whose neck and head seemed one and who told her he had five children who needed "a mama," she had the back of her skirt, the elastic of her panty hose, invaded by the man's moist hand as he said, "I believe Jaysus has brought us together."

She wants to laugh at herself; halfway through a smile the specter of Olney, loose from his high chair, dims the door. He touches Matthew's leg. "Wed?" He points to the toilet paper. "Wed?"

"Boo!" Jeannie says, then, "Blue."

"You like bluegrass?" Matthew asks. Olney's baby talk in her ear, it sounds like he is saying, "Dewed grass." She imagines running through it, barefoot.

"Picking and singing? The music?"

"Sure."

"I could bring my guitar back tonight."

Jeannie thinks of Matthew's battered truck in her driveway, the neighbors. They would talk, have wanted to since the funeral. It is painful how quickly people want something to be over with: William's illness, his death, Olney's babyhood, her widowhood, or, barring that, her respectability. She wants desperately to hear bluegrass, a call from earth almost to say she is still among the living, a woman whose debt to her husband's provision cannot be everlasting.

His mother and father always hinted she was slightly beneath William. She could spend a life trying to live up to their image of her, a realization they in Oregon and William in heaven-knew-where would never see, or she could open her mouth and say yes. Yes to not being alone, yes to the notion she could take care of herself, was herself. Yes?—she asks herself—yes to the attraction of a man, this young man, no to her son who must see he is not her only reason for living.

Death, William's or anyone else's, must always be over, she thinks, must be moving quickly to become the past. The present belongs to those who can make mistakes. The dead have lost the privilege, the talent.

Olney reaches up for Matthew, pulling him down toward him. She resists the symbolism of that, knows her saying yes is her own answer, nobody else's, that she is responsible, a person, Jeannie, not an attachment to the social order, wife, mother, daughter-in-law, lover. When Matthew comes tonight, she knows she will welcome herself as well as him, will entertain herself, embrace herself.

In the medicine chest mirror she sees her face. It is prettier, it seems now to her, a year or two older than its age, and around her eyes, green, her best feature, she sees a certain resemblance to William's face. He loved to tell her how, in the insurance business, there were a number of ways of taking no for an answer: he had to know them so the person who'd said no would know what he meant, really meant to say.

CV10

Walter could almost feel the rush of breath, hear the women roaring, mothers, girlfriends, sisters, sweeping up toward the flight deck, the warm fall day, San Francisco, 1945. A couple chasing a blue jump-suited baby girl just beginning to walk wobbled by him in exaggerated pursuit. He had been alone that day. Hadn't wanted to get off the ship or sleep anywhere but the chain-hung bunks inches above and inches below two other men whose smells and habits he knew better than his own.

He had been seventeen, eighteen the next week. Lt. (jg) Stinson was dead. Three thousand men ("officers and men," they always said in casualty lists as if they died differently) yelled down at thirty thousand skirts, and nobody said anything to him. Buddies he'd held when they were bleeding, buddies who'd cried, told him heart secrets, secrets that still made his cheeks red, buddies had their sea-bags on their shoulders. They'd said good-bye the night before, at the party in the mess, and later in the hangar deck, the warm Pacific melting by, gold in the moonlight, peace, relief a kamikaze wasn't spiraling toward them overwhelming. There would be peace. Friends always. They would remember the dead. In the morning, they'd forgotten all about it.

There had been a telegram for him in the USO clearing station from his uncle and aunt—they lived outside Indianapolis—his mother had died while he was at Marcus Bay and he hadn't known about it for three weeks. The telegram sounded like a message from the president. "Congratulations on a job well done. You are welcome to stop by here a day or so in the absence of other plans." He had wondered, never found out, whether his father was still alive. His father had left his mother when Walter was eleven. A sailor. That was why Walter had wanted to join. Quit high school. Find his father. Or be like him.

Walter's legs trembled walking up the wood steps to the ship's entrance. He remembered the gangways. He'd paid $6.00 to get in, didn't want to ask if there was a discount for veterans who'd served on the ship. The woman ticket seller was in a glass box with a pass-through slot like a drive-in bank teller. "World's largest ship museum."

The hangar deck had been painted a sort of aqua. Walter felt he was in a place he'd lived in his whole life and never been. The first day at sea he'd had to go all the way forward with a stack of flight logs and he'd hugged the wall he was so frightened by motion, huge engines being wheeled along to mechanics' stations, the men in forklifts avoiding collisions only by the roll of the ship as it steamed south, going nobody knew where. The ceiling opened up then and a tennis court–size elevator descended, two F4Us, their wings folded like obedient insects, waiting to be worked on, huge in proximity though Walter had seen them tiny in the sky. This ship was the war. He might be killed. Wounded. That was worse, fliers said who'd already been in the Pacific theater and had come back through Norfolk for rehab or mustering out if they'd been hurt bad—some said "good"—enough.

"Where the hell have you been?" the petty officer who took the logs from him said. "I called you down here forty-five minutes ago!"

Then he got to know people. Men called out to him, "Ears!" Everybody had nicknames, Annapolis custom filtering down to enlisted men. He had mess mates, bunk mates, sick bay where he worked, a plane he was assigned to. When sorties were run, every man had a top-deck station except the engine room crew, and Walter had Stinson's. Walter had a job, a war to win, the scrambled-egg hats kept saying. Not a day went by, not one, not a single solitary day, that he didn't say Stinson's name. "Hey, Buddy," Stinson, officer, gentleman, pilot, told him. "I'll stand up with you when we get back and you head down the aisle."

"Married?" Walter asked. "I might not . . ."

"Hoo! Everybody's going to. And I'll invite you to mine. I'm going to drink so much champagne my blood'll run clear. Hooo!"

Then Stinson, Lt. (jg) Wallace "Whippet" Stinson lifted off the flight deck on his first mission and the flight officer worried the propellers wouldn't catch, the air was so humid: Stinson came back seven pounds lighter. Not one man had been lost; they'd hit Marcus, hit the Japanese planes on the ground, the fueling depot, the port. And Stinson said he was so scared he was sitting in a pool of water in the cockpit and it wasn't sweat. Walter pulled him out of the plane; Stinson turned his face aside so nobody could see his eyes. Only Walter saw them: blank, dead.

The officers were snooty the first weeks out until proximity, dependence, and fear closed the social gap. Stinson was friendly. Walter remembered the eyes: warm, coffee-colored, not so dark they didn't catch the light when he smiled. He told Walter to call him "Whip"—"They'll think you're saying Skip."

"Don't tell anybody!" Stinson gripped Walter's arm so hard Walter thought the young lieutenant's hand—he would always be young in Walter's mind, though he'd been four years older than Walter—would draw blood. Stalking along the flight deck, parts of it covered with linoleum squares now and colored arrows so people wouldn't lose their way on the "museum" tour, Walter felt the wattle under his chin.

"Tell anybody what?" Walter had asked.

"That I'm afraid. That I'm scared. The sky's a poison lake. Every tracer you see means three you don't. You won't even know when you won't even know." Walter thought he was joking, this man, boy, now, who'd been to college, had a girl he was going to marry back home, a boy whose parents sent him money even over his navy officer's pay. "I mean it!" He said he was afraid as much of the other men on the ship as he was of the sky.

"So am I," Walter whispered, but the hours of clamor, the turbines, antiaircraft aak-aak, the earphones, the awful fear of not being able to pick out the sound that would kill you, deafened them. That was their friendship; they could not hear each other, but they talked to each other.

"God, Ears! I can't keep going up the rear end." That was his expression for night flights. "They want you to fly in formation. I'm supposed to be two inches off the wing—worse, *between*— the wing tips of two jerks who're myopic grain-alcohol drinkers. How do they get the stuff? You're not supposed to let it out of the dispensary."

"The head surgeon . . ."

Walter began to find his way, the ladders he'd gone up and down, a monkey, nearly three years, the passage to the lavatory where he'd sat, exposed to the rest of the crew; he saw a couple, their whole appearance a Hawaiian shirt, focusing on a Corsair set up for display, and just as Walter looked at them, simultaneously they touched their crotches, she to brush some ash from his cigarette—think of letting them smoke, here— and he for heaven only knew what reason—and Walter remembered the cook'd put something in the food to keep that part of the body out of the ship's mind.

"I don't want to get you in trouble," Walter had said. "You're not supposed to fraternize." The bronze plaques on the top deck, the "Hall of Fame" that only included officers and industrialists, war fat cats, made Walter furious.

Nobody had ever liked Walter before. He had been the wrong size all the wrong years. Too small for B-team in eighth grade. Too big for Midgets in seventh. The difference between not being popular and not being liked hadn't occurred to him until he got on "The Fighting Lady"—the expressions they had—"So-and-so is still on patrol"—"So-and-so made the supreme sacrifice."

Coming here—the South—was wrong, he thought, the first night. He had walked along the streets and walked, walked, been glad in a way his wife had died; she wouldn't have liked the idea of a pilgrimage to an aircraft carrier. She was younger, too young to remember the war, much else. Stinson hadn't been able to "stand up for him at his wedding." Walter remembered the day. Carlice, his wife, had a bad complexion. She cried and cried the day of the wedding because two big places erupted on her cheek and chin. She put some sort of cover makeup on the spots that only accentuated them. He didn't know how to say that night, as she lay crying beside him in the bed they would share thirty-five years, that it didn't matter. That the heart was somewhere underneath the skin. He had walked, thinking of that, of his daughter who tried to be dutiful though she was, he knew, slightly embarrassed by him. His ears? Job—learned in the navy—male nurse—the years before female telephone linemen, male stewardesses. He kept walking, as if he weren't getting anyplace and yet felt he could go on and on, passing little southern city-gardens. Stinson had had a farm. "Country place. When I fly over these tropical plants I wonder if they'd grow back in the states."

"You better keep your mind on your tail," Walter told him. "You thinking about daffodils."

"Every gunner, every cook, every medic, every clerk-typist is assigned to a pilot and a plane. That's *your* baby! You'll serve that knight like the squires of old! He won't—can't—go into battle without you!" Walter could hear the deck officer lecturing them.

"Kids on the living room floor," Stinson said, "running toy airplanes around on the rug. Varoom, varrooom!"

Walter would wind up the prop on the fighter, thinking any second he was going to get his skull sliced. He wouldn't be the first. Then he'd crouch by the side, or down in the gunneries while the navy-blue plane, wings unfolded, varoomed, varrooomed, Whip standing on the brakes, the other planes beating behind him, Walter hoping the engine was warmed up enough though God knew, in the heat, Alaska should've been ready. Then Walter would watch, his ears stinging, heart banging against his T-shirt, Stinson bump, bump, bump down the deck, over the great number CV10 painted near the end, and hobble off into the sky, the other planes screaming down the line seconds later.

The mission was not a success: the Japanese knew where the fleet was now; hiding behind atolls and steaming zigzag all over the Coral Sea didn't work anymore. Kamikazes were bouncing off every carrier and cruiser. One—a near miss— had been fished out of the water on the starboard: the cockpit had been bolted down from the outside and the dead Japanese pilot's controls had been wired on. "Dumb sucker," Stinson said.

There was a big brouhaha over whether—he looked like a bee with his goggles, helmet, earflaps tight around his chin— the Japanese should be given Christian burial. "Oh, Jesus," Stinson said. "Shoot the works! Who knows who's next?"

He was. Fewer fighters were getting back; those who made it had been through the wringer. The seaman artist who rated a cheer whenever he appeared topside with his rising-sun template to paint Zeros and sunken ships on the quarterdeck vanished. The sick bay was packed. Walter knew the navy hymn by heart from funerals. "Remember the first word in that event," Stinson said.

When Stinson hit the flight deck, it was moments after the Japanese had rained phosphorus over the ship. When you stepped on a piece it burst into flame. Nobody could get to the planes to pull the pilots out of the way. The stop straps were burned through. Walter was helping put a cast on a boy with a broken hip. They had him up on a winch. The cook was painting thick layers of plaster over the body. Walter would've laughed if he hadn't seen the boy's face. The smell of blood-soaked flight jackets cut off bodies mixed with sweat and nausea, the jerk and sway of the carrier as the skipper tried to out-maneuver the fire bombers. People were being sick and nobody had time to mop.

"No, he ain't in yet, Stinson," two medics said who'd brought another body—they thought he was alive—how could you fly in, make a perfect landing, and be dead? "And he probably won't be in. You hear the reports?" He got in. Seventy-eight wounds on his chest, back, legs. Flak. How could he talk? Walter wondered, much less upset than he thought he would be; working, patching up bodies made him think he could save anybody. The chief surgeon took a piece of metal half the size of a bicycle rim out of Whip's face.

"Don't worry," Walter said.

"We weren't the only ones," Stinson said, naked, his body like an ocean with whitecaps only red.

"The only ones?"

"Who were scared."

"Shut up a minute," the surgeon said, and took another metal rim out of his cheek.

"How do I look?" Whip asked.

"Leslie Howard." When Whip tried to smile, Walter saw half his teeth were gone. His face twisted the way a tree turned in strong wind.

He hung on. Walter wrote letters for him, read to him from Saroyan books. Running his hand over the names of the commemorative tablets now—Walter wasn't able to find anything, his battle station, the places he thought he could never forget—he thought those had been the happiest days of his life. Somebody was dependent on him. Somebody spoke to him without saying a word. That sound—the noise between the noises—answered practically every question for him. The present. The war. Friendship. The rest of life. The name finally under his fingers, the block letters pressing into his knuckles, was more painful than any of the past. If the war had ended a different way, Stinson alive, Walter, they'd never have seen each other again. This way they would always be friends. Some men's lives never ended; they kept wandering around thinking something else was coming.

Walter knew it before Stinson. His color. The chief took in Stinson's appearance sideways. The ship news, a legal-size sheet whose inanity was undimmed by casualties, told of more and more victories. The Japanese were "broken" but didn't seem to know it.

The flag didn't go into the water. He knew sometimes parents didn't get the exact flag. Walter thought how hard getting food out to the carrier was, mail off, on, keeping ammunition, parts coming.

The hot wind that boiled the stomach mixed the words: Walter had never liked the chaplain though he'd dragged ten men out of a bulkhead fire, and never, Stinson said, let you forget.

> . . . the Lord,
> who opened . . .
> a path through mighty waters,
> drew on chariot and horse to their destruction,
> a whole army, men of valour . . .
> never to rise again.

They always read that at the dumps. Walter's duties now included, if there was a moment in the bleeding, hauling out the prayer books. The white edges were dirty along the funeral service pages.

> they were crushed, snuffed out like a wick:
> . . .
> Here and now I will do a new thing:
> . . . Can you perceive it?

Walter stuck books—they were always flying off over the rail—in as many hands as could hold them. Four other packages. Whip would've said, "Odd man out." They began with him. Walter couldn't see the splash, to mark the spot in his mind.

The body there, a picture, stayed, a cage like the sunken ships and plane skeletons fish swam through. The boatswain's pipe—Walter didn't know whether he was here or there, now, then—keened. "Now hear this." They were showing a movie forward.

Walter went in, sat down. The dark slowly gave way around him. He remembered going to a show with Whip—one of the things officers, men could do together.

"Nothing makes you forget quicker than a flicker. Well, we

can't get a pint." Stinson's voice was right there, next to him. In the images rolling, in competition with the waves, Stinson whispered, surprised, "I know I'm still on a ship."

Walter stared at the few tourists in the seats. Bored. Squirming. Whispering. They had brought children. The film was a documentary—had won an Academy award. How phony the narrator's voice sounded, false the sailors' smiles, passing down the mess line. He recognized no one though the film was made when he was on the ship. It went on. Walter felt proud, more like these people than the boys who'd squeezed into the theater then, lined the walls, hung from the girders, stuffed the aisles until the fire officer said they had to clear out and a roar of protest sounded to panicky sailors like the air raid warning.

Slowly, Walter took in the steel beams, the X-girders, the superstructure of the flight deck above. He would wait till the end of the movie though he might be the only one left in the theater. He didn't feel as alone, as afraid as he had the day, those years gone, when the carrier docked. He'd go back to the motel—think of having someplace to go—and when the rates went down he might phone his daughter and son-in-law. Or watch television. Go for a walk, see whether he could make out the ship from the other side of the bay.

The Coalition

The phone rang. The phone. Not the alarm clock. Wood was so confused by the profusion of household duties thrust upon him by Gracie and the children's departure that the objects he had dusted and swept around and the spaces he'd vacuumed spoke in mixed voices, the crumb-laden, recalcitrant toaster, for example, mimicking the mailbox when the postman tumbled the lid with junk mail, or the sink disposal pretending to be the toilet upstairs that ran, sending him regularly on a fool's errand to jiggle the handle. These things spoke, not of cooperation but of protest, at being moved, or cleaned, at being deserted by Wood and Gracie, or being imperiled by tenants, people they didn't know, and they didn't stop with speech but acted, reaching out, snagging the Hoover cord, blowing gusts of malicious wind behind the dustpan just when he got everything swept into a vector, or glaring at any possible renter with the awfulness of an unflushed toilet, or a rotten vegetable he could've sworn he'd picked up on the kitchen counter. These things questioned his standing in the community, his moral principles, his personal habits, shouted: How can you live this way?

He had only to shave or shower for the hand basin or the tub to preen itself in soap scum and paradoxical hair—more lost than he'd ever had. Charcoal footprints followed him, *his*, he supposed, the prints of an entire rugby team and their supporters, greasy, bottle throwing, paper trashing. How could one person make such a mess?

When he had volunteered to stay behind and fix up the house to rent until they could find a new one where Gracie had gone with her job, or the housing market changed, he hadn't dreamed how much his wife did.

The phone rang again. "Hello? I don't want to come in," a woman's voice said, adamant. Wood knew her, her occupation, at least: social work, school administration, or political party secretaryship—"good" on the telephone.

Wood said, "You can look around if you like. The outside

doesn't really give an idea of the space." He never knew on these calls whether to say there was more or less than met the eye.

"Just tell me where it is so I can ride by," she said impatiently.

Wood gave the address, directions. Her voice suggested she had heard it all.

He sat down. He looked at the quiet cleanness of the room— the walls he had painted and then stripped because the wall-paper pattern had shown through and then painted again a color Gracie had mailed him the chip of. He had made the room perfect ("within your limits" it protested) for someone he didn't know. Each time he went to the phone or the bath-room or the kitchen he followed his own path, smoothing his prints on the carpet, treading near the edges where the pile was deep and his children hadn't played it thin.

He went to the front door for some air. The house, unheated until then—he could stand anything though it was November— had gotten stuffy when he turned on the heat.

He opened the door, art deco, along with the fireplace-surround, the only visible manifestation of the time when the house was built, and beheld a large behind. A woman was bent over looking into the living room window. She turned on him furiously. "I just want to ride by!"

Wood swallowed. "But come in?" he said. "It's all clean. I'd be glad to show you."

"No! I just want to drive by," she said sweeping past him into the front hall. She put her hands on her hips and looked around. The things in the hall glared back. "It's furnished?" she asked, devastatingly uncertain.

"Partly," he said.

She appeared stunned by such a claim.

("You'll have a hard time renting a furnished house," a real estate agent had told him.)

"May I be frank with you?" she said, leading the way into the living room where she sat down, motioned him to, and took out a cigarette from a jeweled silver case that had a matching lighter attached.

"Dr. Schuster and I expect to be married within the month." She took a deep puff and blew it toward the ceiling. "We will need a larger place. Larger than this!" she said, her eyes, Wood felt, falling on a corner of the floor where steel wool had failed to dislodge splattered paint from a brush he'd dropped. He handed her an ashtray. She looked at the bottom and then settled it on the sofa next to her. Kicking off her shoes, she curled her feet under her.

"Doctor and I have been living together—a deeply satisfying relationship—more than man and wife—nine years. *Nobody* knows it! We've been *that* careful. Now, finally, he's getting a divorce. His wife is an alcoholic.

"No need to say anything," she said as Wood opened his mouth to say precisely that. "Nobody knows it but you. No one! You understand my situation? Your neighborhood's innocuous. Something could be done with this." She indicated, as he thought she would've put it, "the décor." "After we're married—eventually—we'd look for something better, naturally."

She rose, commanding him in her sweep, nodded at a little table, inlaid, his and Gracie's best piece—he was supposed to bring it in the car when he'd rented the house—and began a tour of the rooms.

"Just two baths?" she demanded, upstairs.

"And a half—down—under the stairs," he said, astonished at how years ago, growing up, everybody had managed with one bath, how his mother and father had maneuvered their personal habits out of the range of dinner-table conversation. His own children ran through the house exposed and farting. "What? This house has only two and a half baths?" This house has only twenty-six bathrooms? What did people do in that many bathrooms?

"This might be made into a bath," the woman said, condemning his and Gracie's bedroom. "They're doing that a lot now, putting the tub in the middle of the room, draping the walls with matching fabric." Then she saw it was the best bedroom. "Oh!" She looked deceived.

"Room for a bed and a dresser," he said. "And some dirty clothes." He bent to pick up his pajamas. He had missed them somehow when he made up his bed. The pajamas, given him as a birthday joke at work, had figures in sexual intercourse positions printed on them. He never wore them because of the children or his own modesty but nothing else had been clean.

"I think that's why there's so much divorce these days, don't you?" she said.

"What?"

"Living in a trailer? One of them has to stay in bed to let the other get dressed. I've always insisted on spacious quarters for Dr. Schuster and I."

He stared at her solecism but her moral indignation was more than equal to it. She led, flicking the wallpaper, matching her sleeve against the woodwork, the way downstairs to the living room, took up her place, and lit another cigarette. Her face was flushed, her eyes small but bright. Her body though weighty appeared controlled, a separate unit inside her dress suggesting Lycra, something from researchers at Du Pont.

"Really!" she said, exhausted. "I think it would honestly be better if I started all over. Total new beginning! Clear out the whole thing! Everything!"

With no place to store their furniture, he and Gracie had decided to try and rent furnished. On the other end, they could rent unfurnished. Gracie was clever, he could handyman a fairly comfortable temporary existence.

"I'm into earthtones," the woman said. "This could be attractive with the right accessories. Deep carpet. A big squashy sofa. Downlighters." She put her thumb up as if she were an artist measuring the perspective of downtown Florence.

"Oh!" she said. "I've hurt your feelings! I *am* sorry!"

"No," he said.

"Oh, of course I have!" she said with asperity. "I can tell hurt feelings when I see them! Seventeen years in the public school system, devoting my life to young people, has certainly taught me how to recognize hurt feelings!" She seemed delighted, Wood thought, to recognize such. He winced for her young charges.

"Do you teach?" he asked. He thought the wrinkles that should've been on her forehead from commerce with the young might have been smoothed by her slight excess of weight.

"I know you don't mean to be inquisitive," she said, "but I must insist on your not prying. You can understand, if you're at all sensitive, the vulnerability of my position." She took a deep breath. "Yes, I think Doctor and I will be very happy here. At least for a little while. You'll have to make concessions. I'll have to make them. But then we all will. I wish your wife were here. She'd be so much easier to talk with. You are married? I rather think she's not to blame for some of this?"

She finished her cigarette by somehow making the butt hiss, shushing him when he opened his mouth to say he and Gracie were of one mind. She stood up, smoothing her dress provocatively.

Wood heard the front door slam. He looked out the window and saw her bending over, again the buttocks—he had begun to think of her as a center—to pick an armful of rhododendron boughs from his prize bush. She regarded the bush as if it offended her, after she had denuded it, poked it a few times.

She got into a large car, its metal corroded and torn and bent, quivering in the cold wind. Inside the car was a waspy man, impatient, nervous—had he been there the whole time?—slightly younger than the woman but from the glance, Wood imagined, an even match. He watched them buzz at each other—a hornet searching for a spot, a flesh resisting—before they drove off.

Wood rectified the sofa cushion, took the ashtray to the

half bathroom he hoped had been a redeeming feature, and emptied it.

Then he went outside to look at the rhododendron bush. It no longer seemed his though once he had been happy at its ability to survive the winter green. Back in his chair, he wondered what his feet had brought in; had he missed a call?

The ring was precise. There was no confusing it with any other bell in the house. Wood picked up the phone. The voice sounded young, thin. Speeded up. The caller asked for a time "mutually convenient," the visit would be "minimal," he "knew what he wanted," his "taste was sure."

At the agreed-on moment there was a precise knock. A tap on the glass door insert. Key? Coin? Wood prayed the tap would not crack the glass. *They* would say, "We don't make that kind of glass anymore." What difference did it make that the man was wearing an earring?

He seemed familiar to Wood, from another, fatter world, twice familiar, somehow. Wood stared.

"Something wrong?" the man said. "I'm Doctor—" The way he said "Doctor."

Not quite sure he was speaking or thinking—after living alone these weeks Wood, desperate to be rid of the house but aware it was his life's only accumulation, had to reassure himself—he said, "You were in the car with that woman!"

"I *walk* everywhere I go! Conveyances are killing people. Our legs are being retracted into our bodies. I don't drive, I *won't* drive!

"Actually," the man said, suddenly intimate, "my license was suspended for DUI. I had had a couple. I admit it. The judge said, 'No such thing as *two* beers! Two rabbits! Ha!' Personally, I believe we shouldn't have to endure humor in the judiciary. Justice is serious business. That test they give you's stacked. Smell? My breath's like ocean air." He blew in Wood's face— Wood thought he had swallowed Kentucky.

"Is this the house for rent?" the doctor asked briskly.

Wood remembered the second familiarity. The man *was* a doctor. They had been together on a package tour once. Their families. The doctor had been fatter then. They'd had a good time, their children, with the kind of intensity a ten-day trip can generate, promised to see each other again, which they never did. Wood had heard that the doctor had begun drinking heavily, lost his wife and children and his money and profession, sworn eternal and public vengeance on normal life.

"Your friend who works in the public school system . . . ?"

"She told you she worked for the public school system? What a lot of hooey! Fraud! I'll get her. She's a wino!"

"I've got her mixed up," Wood hastened. "With somebody else. She didn't say anything."

"Yeah? She's a clam," he said with sudden pride. "But she can be prized open." He winked.

"It has four bedrooms, two and a half . . ."

"Never use them! Dogs have to be let out. I go in the morning! Does it leak?"

"It did . . ."

"Oh, everything 'did.' 'Did' put Noah in the ark."

". . . I think I've stopped it."

"Water comes in here, point A, crosses point Q, comes in the house at point Z. Who wants to hear it? Is there a .wine cellar?"

"A basement."

"Temperature constant?"

Wood thought about the washing machine and the dryer and the furnace. "It's constant," he said.

"Are these curtains fireproof? I know: you never tried them!"

He kicked at the baseboard as though it were a tire on a used car lot. Then he thumped the walls. "Plaster? You can have dry wall! Did you know beaverboard was named for Mr. Beaver who invented it? Mr. Beaver! Ha!"

As with the woman, Wood had no need to keep up his end, wondered what different things a house meant to different people. The woman had seen it as a laboratory for experiments in the decorative arts; this man would test its durability, its flammability. A doctor, he had learned to gauge a body's longevity and condition by striking its knees with a hammer, invading dark and forbidden holes with a tongue depressor or some tortuous medical version of a Polaroid camera on a plumber's snake. Was the man even that kind of doctor? The woman would never have said "doctor" that way if he hadn't been.

Wood thought of his and Gracie's life in the house, its space and prewar pretensions that had convinced his children they could compete with their better-off schoolmates. Wood had lucked into the house before real estate boomed. When they bought, the neighborhood was wobbling, winds of escape as well as invasion threatened. Then two interior decorators bought one house. Wood had been astonished by what geraniums in a pot and sixteen percent interest could do. Now Wood hated to sell his house, couldn't afford to stay in it.

"Is there a back way out?" the doctor wondered.

"It has a door out the kitchen and these French windows open. Sometimes," he said, struggling. He had closed them for the winter. Why did they still swell after forty-five years? The man watched Wood banging the top, throwing himself against the jamb, yanking on the handle. When he finally got them open, the man said, "Oh, don't bother opening them for me. I believe you. I think the sun's over the yardarm!"

"The yard?"

"I said, where's the liquor? Never mind." With an unerring instinct the man opened a cabinet door, poured himself a bumper. Before Wood could think what to do, the doctor was on his second.

"I hope you'll excuse me," Wood said, "I have . . . I have an appointment."

"Don't want one? I've had periods of that myself. You look back over your practice—people come in with the damnedest things—you wish you'd told more to go home and have a couple. Side effects minimal. Cheap. Cheaper than pills. Cheaper than me!"

Thinking of the side effects, Wood reached for the bottle. He didn't know whether he was snatching it away from the man or whether he himself was violently thirsty.

"Oh, go ahead! Don't mind me," the man said. "I heard there was a house for rent somewhere around here. You wouldn't know which one, I suppose?"

"This one!" Wood shouted.

"Well? Hadn't you better show me around? I can drink anytime! I mean, I think the sociability of Americans is coming in for some criticism in Japan and the European Economic Community. It's no wonder they're beating the socks off us! And one more for the road!" he said, laying hands on the bottle.

"You've seen it!" Wood said, exasperated. "There're four bedrooms and two other rooms! Two car garage!"

"Oh? You're too modest. I want to see everything!"

Upstairs, he asked where the bathroom was.

"Two. Two and a half, really," Wood said, watching him go into the bathroom. He heard him unzip his pants. Then he saw him, white, somehow winged, sprawl, sliding, wildly loose on the smooth new linoleum floor. Had something been in the whiskey? Wood rushed into the bathroom. Of all his recent friends, the workmen who had done for the house what he couldn't and charged him accordingly, the plumber, the floor people—who to call? Suddenly the man jumped up, straightened his tie, sober as the judge whose humor he had maligned. The swiftness of his motion made Wood grab the wall.

"If I give you $500," the doctor said, "would you hold it for me until Wednesday?" Forever, Wood thought, wondering at the speed at which a happy life—home, job, family—could disintegrate into a couch session with this doctor.

Wednesday, the doctor—Doctor—called and asked whether Thursday would be all right, Thursday, Friday. Saturday, the house shook. Wood looked out to see a U-Haul van striking the oak tree in the front yard. The doctor was directing the tree with the same enthusiasm he had shown for putting down Wood's whiskey. Wood ran out. He saw young men in the cab, flashes of gold in their ears.

"Hey! Look! Can you show me that bathroom again?" Dr. Schuster called. "I tell all my patients, never pass up a watering hole. You shouldn't bottle things up inside."

Wood had thought the man might be a psychiatrist. Should be a patient. Urology had never entered his mind. Schuster didn't wait to be accompanied, grabbed two of the young men.

Wood peered into the van. The big squashy sofa was there. Toys. An MG-B carcass. Parts of motorcycles. A moose head. Wood thought he saw a pair of feet hanging over the edge of the sofa, someone behind the moose head. Two young children about the same age as his and Gracie's, he saw with a pang, were pulling their bicycles out of the tangle.

Wood went back inside where the two youths were measuring the turning of the stairs with a yellow tape. "Catch an end," Schuster said.

"We should talk a minute," Wood told him.

They went into the living room. "I know you think," Schuster said, "I'm sort of a woozie."

"I haven't had to say anything," Wood said, "since you set foot in the house."

"Yeah, I know I kind of talk, but when you've been on the other side of the table as long as I have you've already heard everything, want to get it out before they start."

"You haven't signed a lease. I don't know who's going to be in here. Who are all these children?"

"Oh, the usual. Those kids in the truck are hers. One of mine's measuring the stairs. That Oriental boy's with me on a trial basis. If he gets along with hers."

"Hers?"

Schuster jerked his thumb over his shoulder. The woman— Wood thought of her as the passerby—was being carried across the yard on the big squashy sofa. The sofa was loaded with other "accessories." The bearers set her down to rest.

"Hey," Schuster said, leaning forward. "I drink! Did you know that? The worst thing is I *want* to. I don't hope for anything more than that, a couple before dinner, couple during, a couple after, couple to make me sleep at night. If I wake up? You get the picture?"

"Please," Wood interrupted. "I can't do anything about this . . ."

" 'There're places for this sort of thing,' you mean? I been to them. She's the only person can do anything. She's the *natural* of what I—what people—drink to become. See? We're not violent. Those boys sleep anywhere. Together. Apart? Love? Hate? Half the time they aren't even here. One of them sleeps in that little car body."

Wood felt a curious—was it self-serving?—compassion for this man. The world had done this to him. It hadn't made any sense and he had tried, without thinking, or from sheer perversity, or from the effects of alcohol, to imitate it.

Wood thought of a letter—an axiom of existence—so smeared with errors and emendations it had to be put down in a fair copy before a message emerged that could then be improved on. All at once it seemed to him to be snowing, axioms, a crisscross wind that blew and stung and found vulnerable spots between doors and windows, neck and collars; when Wood looked out, though, the sun was coldly bright; the children, as varied in height as wobbly stacks of coins on a cashier's desk at the end of the day, were leaning and falling, running back and forth, marking their corners just as two hundred miles south and west presumably his own children were staking claims. Who was he to deny these children? He felt anger someone might be denying his. It was one thing to lose a job, he thought. Or a house and its contents, but to lose a way—he couldn't lose his way over finding the right tenant. This man was here, he could pay, he had chattels, children. Gracie could wonder later, by the fireside of their new home, the children gathered around, whether this man or her husband or both were crazy. He fought the house's seeming a sudden security, the fear of being better off now than later, the eternal caution. Schuster and his "wife and children" might be a drug ring. They could do more damage in a week to the house than the year's rent. Instead of being free he might be looking for a magistrate to serve a dispossession warrant. But Schuster's face did not comply with what Wood had read of the dangerous world. He had paid the $500.

The sofa entered the room. Schuster rose and made an elaborate and sweeping bow. The woman—Wood had seen feet—looked up, indignant.

"You could at least have waited until we got things straightened out," she said to Wood as to an intruder. "Are you leaving that little table? You told me he'd be gone by now. Is there coffee? You grind your own, of course? No one knows Dr. Schuster's special blend but I." She smote her forehead. "Those drapes!"

Wood cleared his throat, stood up, saw the foolishness of his being serious, trying to make them understand, but couldn't stop.

"We love this house. You should've seen it when Gracie and I bought it. We had the kids down painting the baseboards. It's our home." He wished he hadn't used the word "love."

The woman rose from the sofa. She was not as tall as Wood but didn't seem to know this, forcing her grander presence on the room. Her bosom, he thought, trying to be prosaic in order to remain sane, was beginning to heave.

"Love? You don't know the meaning! Love! I'll tell you what love is! Your sister's dying, your only sister. She has to have a transfusion and you are the only person with her blood type! You've been ill yourself, desperately ill; you know it's her only chance. You lie there, your blood oozing into her body, drop by drop. You *feel*"—she slapped the aforementioned chest—

"your strength flowing into her, your blood giving her life. You count your own sacrifice as nothing. Nothing! Love? I'll show you love!"

Wood stepped back, slightly fearful. Schuster peered at her. "You don't have any sisters!"

She seemed no more conscious or injured by this reproof than she would've been by Schuster's saying, "Turn left here instead of right, dear." She considered him, Wood thought, as though he were drunk or sober and it was her duty to alter either state. She sat down beside him on Wood's sofa and put her arm around him. "You know nothing of my family." She explained as to two victims of Down's syndrome. "The new bridegroom taking charge!"

The woman got up and began walking around the room, slowly, slowly, and then faster. Wood could tell she was thinking something very important to her whole being but it was not cerebral activity her walk reflected but womanliness. Her breasts appeared to Wood as soft and round as puppies. He could almost smell their milky sweetness. Her hips moved so easily and naturally Wood forgot the affectations of her previous encounter with him.

"My mind has been under great strain," she said determinedly. "I know this will surprise you"—she looked at Wood but he thought she must mean Schuster or one of the collection of souls moving in and out of the house for nothing would surprise him now—"but I am thinking seriously of becoming a priest. More and more women are being ordained. I feel it may be my true calling, the moment my whole life has been leading to.

"There is mounting evidence that Jesus Christ was a woman. A study conducted by a group of leading psychiatrists suggests and doubtless will conclude his teachings indicate he was female. Are you surprised?" she asked coolly.

Both men said no as if it were a very long word without an ending.

"It will take some study. I shall have to overcome the usual prejudices against women in a predominantly male world. You will have less of my time. Can you stand that?" She was still looking at Wood. Wood wanted to tell her he'd like nothing better.

"Giving blood may have brought me to it," she said. "The room in which I lay had a crucifix hanging on the wall, not just an ordinary one, a cross and human figure created exactly to scale. I asked one of the nuns and she confirmed my deductions. I gave my blood for another, just as He did, and the thought kept pounding in my head that I was that figure hanging on the wall. Do you know what they give you after you've given your blood?" She stopped in front of Wood. He could only think of men and women patients meeting and falling in love in insane asylums.

"Jello! Jello! Bowls of it! Red and purple and orange. The colors of blood!"

"Show him your ring," Schuster said.

She put out her hands which Wood saw were beautiful, pure and white, no hint of liver spots or ever having done any work. They reassured him. The diamond was large and clear. It wasn't just the money; the stone separated notions from practice; he was on the side of gab. He saw the two sons tilting the MG-B body through the front door.

"Hey! You can't put that in the house!" he cried.

"Oh," the woman explained, "they're doing the most exciting things with *objets trouvés*. I wish I could take you to this year's Decorators' Showcase, really go around with you, piece by piece. I suppose there isn't time?"

What was to stop her, Wood wondered, at mere earthtones at the whole earth lay out there before her?—to be brought in, redistributed in the house.

The boy who'd helped carry in the sofa took a box of framed photographs from the sofa seat and began placing them around the room. One of the little children tooled in on his bike and gave Schuster a fat envelope. He opened it and handed Wood half again the amount he'd asked for. "You got a lease?"

Wood went to the desk drawer and took out a form-lease he'd bought at the stationery store. He had crossed out certain clauses, written in stipulations during his loneliness, wondered at how airy an airtight lease still might be. Schuster read it more carefully than Wood thought a lawyer was capable of. He had written in that the house would have to be available for showings after April first if he, the landlord, decided to sell it. The showings would be at the convenience of the tenants. "Could we say no more than once a week?" Schuster asked, perfectly reasonable.

"Not Mondays," the woman said, "I hold 'at homes' then to help troubled youths. Home's so much warmer, so much more cordial than the office space at school, don't you think?"

"Oh stop it!" Schuster said. "Say, you know?" to Wood. "You're beginning to look more and more familiar." One of the sons put a gigantic Stilson wrench on the little inlaid table.

Wood thought of how he'd surprised Gracie with it when she hadn't wanted to be pregnant and he hadn't wanted her to be either. It was a great extravagance, and they had eaten on it that night, very close, before the fire; she'd made her favorite dish, shrimp gumbo, and his, which he couldn't remember or which had changed, and they had started weeping, Gracie saying over and over it was all right for a man to cry, and Wood wondering where to buy a high chair, imagining it would cost as much as the antique table.

"Don't worry," Schuster said. "They always lay a dropcloth."

Wood quickly counted the money, squeezed by the MG body in the hall, and began to take things out to his car. He figured he could be finished packing and gone in an hour if he didn't stop to grind coffee beans. He would leave the little table. The woman had put a silver-framed photograph on it of an emaciated-looking woman who could easily have been a sister, he thought, with some rare blood type.

Every Known Diversion

Paul and Herbert are running along the levee. Herbert is tall, but Paul is a doctor. They have been best friends and runners together since high school.

They begin to speed up, neither knows why—usually it means one has something to tell the other—as they reach the fort where the English founded the city in 1707. Both of them have been to so many historical society meetings they imagine they were here at the time. The river on their left, once muddy from erosion but now cleaned up by a federally funded dam both of them fought, and the canal on their right, dug in the early nineteenth century to provide power for the mills by Chinese laborers whose descendants run the restaurants that are so much a feature of the city, sandwich the two men between water-cooled breezes. "Penny and I are splitting up," Herbert says.

Paul is hurt because as best friends—almost, to hear their wives tell it, they're same-egg, time-in-the-womb-together best friends—he hasn't divined or suspected anything. He turns his head, increasing his stride, and looks up at Herbert as a doctor, searching for some medical reason.

"Why?"

"More reasons, *she* says, than *she* can explain," Herbert tells him.

"Does it have anything to do with Mindy? I thought that was over and Penny forgave and forgot?" Paul asks.

Herbert keeps his running shoes and shorts in his car and if he and Penny are at a party where he is bored—"No thought of whether he bores us!" some of his hostesses have said—he jogs home alone, anxious to show off his legs and his mobility, his freedom to go from place to place without depending on a machine or gasoline. When the Arab oil embargo was imposed he said, "This won't affect me."

"It doesn't have anything to do with Mindy."

"Well, what?"

"It has something to do with Sally."

"Who's Sally?"

"A girl I've been going around with."

Paul thinks sometimes when Herbert tells him he has been "going around" with a girl while he is married that he is listening to a patient who shouldn't be wasting time with a urologist but should be seeing a psychiatrist.

Herbert is a lawyer who teaches economics in a small college that is part of the state's university system. Paul asked him once why he gave up practicing law, suspecting there was another reason besides the collapse of Herbert's first marriage. For a moment Herbert's eyes darkened and Paul saw images of family fights over teaspoons, women accusing men, children being asked to decide between parents, people taking the stand and swearing to tell the truth and not bothering to. So Herbert passed into teaching—he is okay for money, good at managing an inherited portfolio and keeping expenses down. What worries Paul is Herbert's womanizing; it isn't as if that is the only refuge from courtroom battles over petty objects or the boredom of academic life. Herbert is a champion of recreation.

"I was going to tell you about her," Herbert says, puffing. His long legs could make one of Paul's two steps but he is usually the first to get winded. "I was going to break it up but I miscalculated."

"Is Penny determined?"

"As much as I am."

"What's that mean?"

"That I'm tired."

"Of her?"

"I'd say of everything, but the remark would make me dislike myself more than I already do."

"How could anybody be tired of Penny? She's a great spirit, fun, down to earth, smart. What else? You sound like you're trying to act bored because you got caught."

"Yeh," Herbert says, his upper lip apologetically overbiting his lower, a gesture Paul knows Herbert thinks is heavy with charm.

"You want to cut it short?" Paul asks as if the news has affected their wind.

"Yeh," Herbert says, turning around. They are working up for a mini-marathon next month to benefit their sons' school.

"Any chance I could talk—to her?"

"No."

"*Anything* I can do?"

"I don't—won't have anyplace to live after the first. She wants the house. And the furniture. And the car. And alimony. And the children!"

"What's she leaving you?"

"Payments."

Paul looks up at his friend, thinks of making payments and making out, Herbert's specialties. "You can stay in the basement apartment at the house, if you want. The med student's leaving."

"The one you call the 'Watchdog'? Why?"

"*You* called him that. He didn't make the grade. Watched Anne, you said, while I was mining kidney stones and watched the house while we were on vacation."

"It seemed a good idea, then," Herbert says. "I humbly believe, Doctor, I could do the same thing. What would Anne say?"

"She despises you, of course!" Paul says, falsely gruff. He knows Anne likes Herbert with the kind of sympathy a mother has for a child's skinned knee, and for the genre of skinning knees, falling while playing. She doesn't take him seriously, even his market tips, which considerably enrich Paul, or his confidence in himself as being irresistible to women. She says that his conquests have some flaw, that plastic surgery instead of sexual license might help, hinting that his women are ugly. Paul wonders if she is unconsciously setting herself up as a pinnacle for Herbert to try to scale. She never asks him for dinner when she has a few people, only for big parties. She likes him, she tells Paul, because he is his best friend and that falls into the same category as their own political differences—they, she and Paul, can talk about things without making each other mad or breaking down into an ultimate sort of Chappaquid-dick vs. Watergate argument.

"She doesn't take me seriously. That's the meanest thing a woman çan do to a man," Herbert says. He starts to run faster, leaving Paul slightly behind.

They often do this—one speeds up and waits at the car. But now they begin to race. Herbert's long legs stretch out almost parallel to the ground. Paul's, blond and hairy, thickly muscular, barely leave the ground. The car is a good mile farther. Neither one seems ready to quit or slow down. Herbert lives on pastry. Paul forces himself and his friends to subsist, at least two days a month, on carrots and bran. Sometimes he believes his and Herbert's friendship is based on mutual indulgence and mutual reform.

Herbert seems to want to lose Paul, seems sorry he has told him about the divorce, sorry to have had to ask for a place to stay. Paul, fighting to keep up, wants to show him he shouldn't be sorry. Paul needs a close male friend, someone tall and successful with women to make him feel better about being short and awkward and spurned by women at parties. He wants to point out the holes in Herbert's makeup to strengthen his own composition. But he is good for Herbert, too, he wants to say, a return when he drifts, an endurable level of boredom to demonstrate to Herbert that he can live with it, that there are worse things. Paul gulps great breaths of air he imagines his small lungs can't handle. His not wanting to give in even when he sees one of them should—men their age die of coronaries—makes him wonder at the absurd things he'd risk life for.

Herbert, his head high in the wind, supposes he has left Paul. They have never raced before, never competed on any ground except scoffable charity runs—"The Faster Pastor," a 10-K to raise money for a burned Methodist church. Their good humor toward each other inevitably prevents a clash. Paul can sense Herbert's bad side a mile off, is skillful in bringing out Herbert's best, as Herbert is in deflating the "I'm a doctor" stuffiness of Paul on occasion. Neither asks the other to be grateful. They like each other, pure and simple. Paul's wife has said to Penny with whom she is not friends, "In the sense that all the world loves a lover, no one can be angry about Paul and Herbert's friendship."

Paul pulls a short foot in front of Herbert. Herbert is astonished to see him, has a sudden vision of his friend catching up with him on a motorcycle. For a second, Paul is ahead. Then Herbert comes down fast and they run dead heat to the end of the levee where they have to stop for the wooden stairs that lead down to where they've parked the car. Herbert is just ahead but not enough to give him the sense of winning or Paul the sense of losing. Out of breath, the future together, the race makes them both feel very good.

"Annie?" Herbert is talking to Paul's wife on the telephone. "I know he said it would be all right but I thought I better call you."

"He's the boss," Anne said.

"You say that like 'he's the boss and I have to do what I don't want to because he is.'"

"Herbert, why do you always insist on this reassurance? 'You can get a lot done in this world if you don't insist on the credit.' You've heard that? A Jesuit motto. The president uses it—when he's taking credit for something."

"You don't sound elated over my arrival."

"Herbert, really! We're delighted you're coming. You'll have complete privacy. We'll probably never see you."

"Is that an invitation to be invisible, never to come upstairs? And why this 'we'?"

"Herbie. If you were involved, say, in the arts, this sensitivity would have a place. Come! We're—*I'm*—delighted to be of help."

"On a charity footing, now?"

"*Come*, Herbie. If it makes you feel better you can do windows and mow the lawn and unstop toilets."

Herbert arrives. Watching him from upstairs—the *piano nubile* Anne calls the main floor of the new Victorian-style house Paul, an only child, bought without her seeing it because he told her it had lots of room for the big family they were going to have—she is amazed at how much equipment Herbert has for diversion. Rackets, skis, bowling balls, bicycles, hockey sticks, golf clubs, croquet sets, mountain climbing gear, fishing rods and reels—every known recreation is represented—butterfly nets, insect specimen boxes, aquariums, scuba diving things. Anne thinks she is seeing a child, a boy let loose in a sporting goods store. There are several cases of books. She squints to see the titles. Tom Swift.

Everything is perfect. Three is not a crowd.

A month goes by, swiftness matched by pleasure. Anne is surprised one evening—the exquisite hour—when Paul says with the air of one who hasn't found satisfaction at home, "I'm going out!"

She looks up from the petit-point spectacle case she is working for his mother. Their two—not so many after all, or many-seeming—children were at camp; she has resisted, so far, without really hurting his feelings, Paul's attempts, his "40s approach" he calls it—he puts on his old Glenn Miller "Pennsylvania Five Thousand" record, his pajamas with the frog closings—to "make another baby." She has cleaned out closets, found things, gotten more done in the month since Herbert's arrival than she feels she has in the last two years.

They have been going to Chinese restaurants and taking recipes home. Anne is wild about eating lilies, devours the garden, the roadside, munching on buds. Paul tells her, "You spend $8.50 for some of those bulbs"—"Tubers," she corrects—"and you eat the buds before you even see what they look like."

"Oh, let her alone," Herbert says. "Taste one!" Paul looks at them as if he is an intruder in the naming and tasting pleasures of the original pair in the garden.

Why, Anne thinks, looking at her husband's petulant face now, has she gotten so much done? Because, she has decided, she always has someone to talk to. She never has to *long* for company, call somebody, or pine for a friend to ask a stupid question to while listening to stupid answers.

Herbert is teaching only two summer school courses. The college is five blocks away. He jogs there in the morning, comes home full of his students' solecisms. He bought a bushel of peaches the day before. He and Paul and Anne mashed them up and churned a gallon of ice cream, made of pure cream, cream colored, not the white coconut-preservative-flavored cream in cartons from the supermarket but pure cream from the farmer who grew the peaches. Wild honey sweetened the ice cream. They downed the entire gallon, went out and bought five half-pints of raspberries, and made another gallon. Herbert rubbed their bellies after and made Anne and Paul do thirty sit-ups. When she got cramps he put her in the hammock underneath the linden trees and played to her on his guitar. His voice was perfectly natural—unlike so many people's singing voices that were different from their speaking voices—and just bad enough to stand Paul's singing along. She watched Herbert's Adam's apple bobbing up and down and touched her own throat. Paul said he was leaving on the second verse, drawn by the *New England Journal,* always as strong in his leisure time as the moon pulling the ocean. Anne looked at Herbert sitting on the grass beside the hammock and realized she was falling not in love but in friendship—which was worse. She thought of Louis XV's still loving Madame de Pompadour when he began to tumble younger mistresses and how the Pompadour had gone around Versailles changing all, well, thirty percent, of the marble goddesses-of-love to goddesses-of-friendship. Anne applied for a grant, January, in sculpture, hoping to do something to fulfill the promise of her old life, to do something worthy of a doctor's wife, but her application was turned down.

The loaded air—the lindens were in bloom and the bees

argued with the drowsy scent as to who could put her to sleep faster—lay upon her, the summer equivalent of a down comforter. In the pleasure of friendship she felt something more overwhelming than sexual fulfillment. As she closed her eyes, she thought it was better. She had nothing to reproach herself with, nothing to regret or to be tired of as she sometimes had with Paul. She heard Herbert's voice, "If summer didn't stop and you came after." It was a song he'd written: "God!" she thought, "if his students could hear that!" She wriggled her toes.

"I'm going out," Paul says again the next night, staring past her through the long floor-length windows to the yard where Herbert is hosing down the sails of his little boat. He is in his bathing trunks and as he leans into the work Paul thinks of some ancient sculpture, a little too posy, Roman copy of a Greek original. He thinks Herbert is aware of his posture, is not doing it for anyone, only his own pleasure.

"And I'll be gone tomorrow, I think," Paul says. "There's a paper I'd like to hear read at the AMA regional in Columbus. Some of the urology department's going, too. We'll just stay downtown tonight. We can sleep in some of the residents' beds so we can get up tomorrow morning early."

Against the possibility of a reflex Anne glances out at Herbert. He has been teaching her and Paul to sail. She loves it, the air, the spitty little waves at the lake. Paul finds it too much trouble, the trailer, the launching, the cleaning up after, the food they have to take, no place on board to pee.

"The beds will be empty?" Anne asks. She and Herbert have gone alone twice to the lake with Paul's knowledge and once without.

Paul says, "You'll be all right?" When they were first married, they agreed never to go anywhere without the other. She thinks he is referring to this.

She says, "I release you from your pledge."

Paul looks at her. He walks over to the easy chair where she is sitting, her bare feet up on an ottoman, the yarn and needles and scissors spread out under her legs. He takes up the brightly colored little case for his mother and puts it close to his eyes. "I thought you were going to make her a pocketbook."

"I was. Herbert needed something for the uncle who's so old to give the aunt who has Meunière's disease on her birthday so he asked for what I'd started. I told him I'd finish it for her and make something else for your mum."

"Something smaller?" Paul asks.

"Something else. I really put my heart into the pocketbook. My own design."

"So you gave it to Herbert."

"Well, to his aunt. She's had a mastectomy. He's really hard hit by this divorce thing. Penny's taking everything."

Paul's face turns the way it did the day, running, Herbert told him he was getting a divorce and he was hurt because he hadn't guessed any of it. "Well, so long!"

"Give us a kiss," Anne says, pulling him down, unwillingly, she thinks, to her lips.

Anne naps, wakes, looks at the little enamel clock on the mantel, rubs her back against the cool cloth of the slipcover thinking how comfortable she is. She gets up, turns on the radio. For once the college station is playing music instead of talking. She wants to sleep again but hates to miss any of this time. She writes three postcards, one to each of the children at camp, one to her mother-in-law. The cards are of French impressionist paintings. She bought them at the museum. She thinks of the artists freeing art forever of sacred subject matter. She thinks of seeing something and holding it. She chooses a Fantin portrait for Paul's mother. She takes up the needlework and pulls a lavender strand of wool into two parts to make it small enough for the openings in the canvas. She thinks she will call Herbert to come up—she has only to tap the pipe by the mantel, a water pipe no longer in use but saved by Paul to prevent the plaster ceiling from having to be ripped up when the pipe was removed. Anne looks up at the ceiling. The house, built by an eccentric contractor less than twenty years ago who wanted to duplicate the house he grew up in, once frightened her—it defied leveling and housekeeping. There was always too much to do. But she has been able to put anything she wants in the house, as have Paul and the children. Not one of her friends says she has any taste. She regards it as a compliment. The friends have had decorators who get in violent arguments with them and charge for mistakes.

Anne taps the water pipe. The door opens immediately from downstairs. "Did you just tap?" Herbert asks.

"You must have been waiting at the door!"

"I wasn't waiting. I was already on the stairs. Ready for our 'shew.' Where's the Daddy?"

They have called themselves an extended family comedy hour, pretending first Herbert is Anne's lover, then Paul's, then one of the children's, Andrea who is ten, and finally the Bouvier des Flandres who looks like a bear and is supposed to be so good with children but has bitten every member of the family.

"He went out," Anne says. "He's going to an AMA conference tomorrow."

"Oh hell, it's no fun without him."

"Thanks a lot."

"Well, Mommie. You're fun but you can't cheat at poker with a straight face. What's on TV? Shall we eat our weight in cholesterol while he's not here?"

He turns off the radio—it is lushing through Saint-Saëns's *Samson and Delilah*—and switches on the portable TV set on the coffee table. Paul will not let the TV be in the living room—"We'd watch it all the time"—but they brought it in to watch the tennis matches and it seems it may stay.

"Reruns," she says.

"But I love them," Herbert responds. "Do you know I never saw *MASH*? I 'missed' the seventies or was it the sixties—whatever they're always saying. The kids were having the eye operations and the leg in a brace and before that I was in Vietnam."

"You *were MASH*," Anne says. "Or was that Korea?"

Herbert brightens. "I was, sort of. Paul says they're taking older people in medical school. Should I go?"

"Sure! Seriously?"

"Semi."

"Soldier, lawyer, professor. You need more?"

"Meaning I should concentrate. Well, I didn't get killed in SEA, I wasn't sued for malpractice and I have a no-hands-on policy with nubile students."

"Do you think *I* should go to medical school?" Anne asks. "I majored in chemistry. The trouble is you have to do it more than once. The brain. I'd love to get in there once, inside the skull, stir those sluggish gray snails. Twice, I'd resent them. Joking. I majored in applied arts."

"Why don't you turn the air conditioner way up and we'll make popcorn? I'll build a fire? Unpopped popcorn is high, did you see, on the list Paul has for unrefined carbohydrates? It's actually on the list. You suppose anybody actually eats *unpopped* popcorn?"

"Paul is obsessed with roughage," Anne says. "He asks strangers in the airport to swallow these red markers and call him 'when they see them again.' One man called the airport police."

They pop corn in an old screen box Anne somehow puts her hands right on in the utility room. They watch an interminable movie—Herbert calls it a "flim" in honor of the national pastime of "flim-making"— about a girl who married an Englishman whose jealous sister turns out to be, in the remote part of the country where they go to live, a witch or a vampire. Herbert sits on the floor in front of Anne's chair, and when the actress in the movie discovers her panty hose have been chewed up and spit out by what she discovers is a bat, he grabs Anne's bare feet and tries to eat them. There is more—a little more—he puts his hand inside her top, flat on her stomach, grazes her breasts with his other hand. She giggles over the plot and her tickled feet just as Paul, a hugely wronged expression on his face, bursts into the room. His mouth forms to say "A-ha!" but nothing emerges.

Herbert looks up, startled. Anne says, "Where's your car? We didn't hear you come in."

Paul is too embarrassed to admit to himself what he's done. He went to their favorite Chinese restaurant to eat. There was no regional AMA meeting. He ordered something made with lily flour. He tries to blame it on Chinese food syndrome. He left the car in the parking lot and tiptoed, literally, he reminds himself blushing, back the mile and a quarter to the house imagining he would catch his wife and his best friend.

"Oh, Paul!" Anne says very low. "You didn't think—so much for medical school—you *did*!"

She looks down at Herbert for whom she slowly feels a definite sexual attraction. He is wearing pink seersucker shorts from "Polo by Ralph Lifshitz"—"That's his real name," Herbert has told her—"that cost sixty dollars and are coming apart at the seams." Herbert returns the look. He feels a longing for Anne—more of a longing for not having been married twice—a longing for Anne *and* Paul's singularity. They have resisted each other, he and Anne, not from any moral strength but because the pleasure of not consummating the relationship is so excruciatingly sweet. He has loved the days with Anne—and with Paul—more than any time he's ever had. Penny's idea of "at home" was "to go out." During the day when he came home between classes, Penny squinted at him as if he were committing a felony in the male domain and rushed out if she weren't out already, grabbing the children if they weren't already at, between, or on the road to an "activity." Once, when he suggested children need time to be by themselves, she rumbled something about their "peers" and "not getting left behind." When Anne faced something like that with her children, she said, "Piers the Ploughman!"

Paul shuts off the air conditioner, takes a vase of day lilies, and dumps them on the floor, an expression of pain shading his face. Herbert coughs at the smell of burned popcorn. Paul leaves the room.

"I've never burned any in my life," Herbert says. "I guess I'll go back downstairs." He thinks he should've spent more time preparing his lectures for classes. It has not been fair to his students. He does not look at Anne, but when he is behind her where she can't see he opens his mouth till his lips almost touch his ears. He doesn't know whether he's giving his birth-of-an-egg howl to Anne or to Paul.

With the air conditioner off, Anne sits for a long time in the living room feeling very hot. Paul is naturally parsimonious about turning off lights. His favorite saying when they are all in the car ready to go somewhere *en famille* and he sees lights burning in the children's room is "Who's working for the power company?" and he sends them back into the house while he blows the horn. He wants to teach them a lesson. She realizes the futility of trying to teach anybody a lesson. Her instinct to put Paul at some kind of ease over his blunder is discouraged by his not having believed in her or his best friend, having been so paranoid, simpleminded. She wonders about men, what they think of women. He should've known she'd tell him. When she thinks more about it, it seems to her he has even tried to set them up, his own little Abscam. He wasn't enjoying the pleasure of time spent together; he was just waiting. Goose-bumps rise on her arms and legs in the oppressive heat. Herbert and Paul have closed both the doors that lead to the hall and the porch where the breeze comes from. She thinks about the danger of daring to consider happiness harmless, about the game she has played without realizing she was playing. It didn't occur to her that as long as she or Herbert or Paul didn't violate the rules between players a bystander might still be injured, that any one of them could become a bystander, or that

Paul would ever become an umpire since he paced off the boundaries. It was he who was always urging her to like Herbert. "For me," he said.

Paul stands in his room, *their* room—the happiest time in his life was a Sunday morning, two weeks ago, when the three of them, the three people he loved most, got into the big poster bed and read the funnies aloud. Anne brought up cups of coffee and a basket of oranges they peeled, spitting the seeds at each other. Each time they touched each other they drew back in a kind of high parody of sex. Paul especially did not try to hold Anne in a way to show that she was his and that Herbert had nobody.

Paul thinks of being an only child and wonders if it is a status he subconsciously wants to maintain, even now. He remembers, a little boy, hearing his father say to his mother, "I'm leaving you," and her saying, not as interested as he thought, still, she should've been, "Why?" The "why?" had a kind of drifty sound he still threw after everything that ever happened to him. His father said, "I want to get this country into the war! They say, 'It's over there!' It's not. It's right here!" It was. Still in that room. Paul's mother looked around in her vacant way. He remembered the loneliness, the room after his father was gone, his mother's turning in on herself, the way the furniture seemed to shrink, because he was growing, he thinks now, or was there really a withdrawal in which even things, objects, furniture, would have nothing to do with him?

He thinks of running along beside Herbert, of being shorter and being almost—a little taller—on a level with the paps of his chest, of his touching Anne's breasts, of the original cell they all came from, leaving these useless clay-colored moons on the male's chest, the moment, millions of years before, when the cell split that separated male from female, the moment, god or evolution knew when, when what made Herbert Herbert and Paul Paul divided, and how the cell had such an attraction and yet such a resistance.

Paul is embarrassed to think of Herbert before he thinks of Anne. He wonders as he lies down in his clothes, trembling a little, whether Anne will come upstairs, whether Herbert will ever come up his stairs again.

He imagines Herbert folding Anne in his arms, whispering, "He blames us, why not take full credit? Be hanged for a sheep not a lamb."

Paul wonders whether he has remembered to lock his car, parked in the Chinese restaurant lot, his new *JAMA* and *New England Journal* on the back seat; he wanted to read them tonight aloud to Herbert and Anne in a pompous doctor-voice he hoped would convince them he could always be Daddy in their diversions.

Learning Italian

Bea is eighteen. She is a freshman at IU. On Monday her stomach hurts and she skips class. Tuesday, she wakes up surprised to feel better and stays in bed to enjoy the feeling.

Wednesday, she hurries to class. But her watch is ten minutes slow and she is late besides. When she gets to the language arts center where her Italian class meets she sees the clock. Twenty-five after ten. A quarter of an hour late. She is too embarrassed to go in, spends the rest of the hour in the student union drinking a coke and playing Shawn Phillips.

Her other classes are Shakespeare, anthropology, and creative writing. "Good God," her father who won for his age group (fifty-four) in the Chicago Marathon says, "when I was in school we took chemistry, trigonometry, ROTC, and Latin." Bea stares at him through her own disappointment in college, wonders if she would get more out of it, find some meaning in it, if she took harder subjects.

Thursday, Bea discovers her roommate in the dorm where she lives has a boy, or a long lump in her bed. Bea is afraid he—or it—will see her naked as she crosses the room to her dresser to get her pajamas. The lump is a boy. He beckons to her to get in bed with them. She runs from the room, down the hall. Two boys, naked, one very hairy, one very smooth, Jacob and Esau, emerge from the showers. She grabs her clothes, spends the night prowling around the campus, thinking of boys, of how she can want them and not want them at the same time.

There is no point in going to class Friday. She is too tired. Too much to explain, she thinks to herself. Her stomach begins to hurt. She goes to the infirmary doctor, who says, "Young lady, you've got a tiger in your tank. Here, take these."

"What are they?" she asks.

"Nothing much. I don't know the name—these patents run out every seventeen years. Don't worry. I take it myself—my wife takes them. Kids."

"How many?"

"Whenever you get the rumbles. No more than, well, five or six a day."

Bea takes four, feels better, goes to see her sister who is married to a clergyman, lives in a trailer with her thirteen-month-old baby.

"Robert's going to quit the church," Pat tells Bea.

"I didn't think he ever got into the church," Bea says, picking up the baby.

"They have too many people and not enough pulpits. He's mad at God."

"He could take some of these," Bea says, handing her sister the pills the doctor gave her. "They're good for anything."

"Where did you get them?"

"The university doctor."

"This university needs a doctor. They said last night by the year 2000 enrollment in liberal arts will be off twenty-five percent. All those PhDs. All those students. Nobody wants that kind of college education anymore. Doesn't do you any good. What's Plato to a computer?"

"Don't be depressed," Bea says.

"I'm not depressed, but Zanne is."

Zanne is Bea's second sister. She is a junior at IU, goes with Umberto, an Italian boy Bea thinks is the handsomest boy she's ever seen, who has curly hair on his head and creeping up around his throat. Zanne likes to run her fingers through his hair whenever Bea is around. When he comes to visit Bea's house in Indianapolis he pretends to stay in the spare room, but when Bea's parents are asleep, he gets up and goes to Zanne's room. Zanne is so in love she wants to drop out of school. Bea wants to, too. Pat already has.

"You'd make a good poster for the Stay-in-School Society of America," says their father.

"Umberto'd make a good poster," Bea says tugging at Umberto's hair. "It's not fair, looks."

Bea loves her father, his height; he will never be dumpy, the way women get. He has power over his health and physique.

She feels good, hoping she will be like him when she is his age, but when he asks her to go jogging with him, she either drops out the first quarter mile or begs off. She has heard, "All women marry their fathers," wonders, if Pat marries him, and Zanne and herself, what will be left. Where does her mother come in? Looking at her father, her mother says, "Men get better looking, and better; and for what?" She giggles. "I'll out-live him ten years and I don't even know how to pronounce Adidas!" Bea wonders how they found each other, marvels at the way a marriage can work out, wonders why they love her, love Zanne, Pat. All that love. She has done nothing to make them proud of her. How will she find somebody?

Zanne tells Bea she is preggers, says it just that way. "Oh happiness!" says Bea.

"Not so," Zanne tells her. "Umberto doesn't want a bambino."

"Oh, God," thinks Bea. Pat's husband, who didn't want their baby, now loves it. "What are you going to do?" she asks her sister.

"A," she says.

"Where?"

"There's a place in Chicago."

"There's a place here," says Bea, who reads the ads in the student newspaper.

"I don't want it done here. You have to go home and lie down afterward. Somebody has to baby me. I wish I could tell mother. I can't though. Will you come with me?"

Zanne has always been a flasher, Bea thinks, a beautiful girl who wears makeup and understands the reason for wearing it, to make something already fine unbearable. She has never needed Bea, who is plain though she has big breasts; Zanne doesn't need her now. But Bea wants to go with her because she has never seen an A clinic, thinks it would be a good thing to know about either for her roommate's use or for a novel she might write someday.

They leave for Chicago on the Greyhound. Umberto declines

to accompany them, which sets Zanne off. "You'll drown the bus," Bea says.

"The bastard!" Zanne shrieks so loud the bus driver turns around. "Love goes a long way toward not getting you anywhere," she says bitterly, staring out the window at the breadbasket of the world.

Bea looks at her sister sadly. Imagines she is thinking: one less mouth to feed.

In the city they get a motel room and go to the clinic. The waiting rooms are full of women with babies and older children. "They do that on purpose to make you feel guilty," Zanne says.

"Do you?" Bea asks.

"The pain will relieve the guilt." Zanne has to pay the money in advance. The doctor examines her and asks her questions Bea, who goes in with her, imagines he already knows the answers to. They are to come back the next morning early. Bea thinks of the doctor, who looked vaguely like her father, thinks of the doctor approaching hundreds of women this way. If the two men ever met, would they say how hard it is to raise daughters compared to sons?

In the middle of the night, after Bea eats a hamburger and drinks two beers, Zanne wakes up and says to her, "When you were a little girl, did you think more things would just be, just happen, I mean, naturally?"

"I'm asleep," Bea says.

"Stop it," Zanne says.

"When I think of all the women who want babies," Bea says. "We could have it and sell it?"

"What you mean 'we,' White Man?" Zanne asks.

No one speaks for a moment, then Zanne says, "I mean did you think you would just get married and have babies and have somebody love you and they'd never wet their pants? Everybody would be housebroken and time would be like a dog that came when you called it?"

Bea says, "I'm still asleep."

"I didn't know sex was something else, that it was power and somebody could have it over you and that it was so good you didn't mind being overpowered."

"Mrs. Doctor Corbett says when she was pregnant with Bobby, who's now finishing medical school and is the most wonderful boy I ever knew, her friends said, 'This is the worst time to have a baby, your mother's sick, your father's dead, your husband, if he was indeed that, just went down in Korea, you have to work, go to school, pay a sitter, rent, and tuition. You better buy the coat hanger!'"

"I hate Bobby Corbett," Zanne says. "He's the most self-centered, smug dumbhead I ever knew."

"A difference of opinion at the Holiday Inn Motel at 1:37 A.M.," Bea says, pressing her digital watch and thinking Bobby Corbett whom she loves—from afar—is the ideal boy in her lifetime vision; he is probably not thinking about either one of them at this very hour.

"You're so smart, little sister. I wish this was happening to you," Zanne says.

"It is, it won't, and good night sweet prince," Bea says, mock snoring.

Bea hears Zanne's breathing, fitful, interspersed with little cries. "Sleep," she says out loud, testing the depth of Zanne's repose, "is a contagious disease." She remembers seeing yawns in her college classes, then beginning herself. Now she has caught Zanne's wakefulness. She goes into the bathroom. A mirror over the toilet throws back her reflection in the mirror over the hand basin, infinite times, catching her in what she knows is somebody else's troubles. She wonders why she couldn't have stayed up all night studying, the way she is staying up all night tonight. She wonders, standing in front of the toilet, what it's like to be a boy, urinate upright. She sees in her face, getting smaller with each repetition, the baby's face. It has delicious espresso-brown eyes, thick curly hair, like Umberto. A campus organization she joined because her counselor said she should belong to something opposes political prisoners, torture, the death penalty. She and a friend saw an anti-abortion billboard with a picture of Jesus, finger raised, the caption, "Thou shalt not kill, call such and such a number." Bea and her friend called and asked the people to support opposition to the death penalty. "No," they said, "that's a different thing." Now she thinks it is a different thing. Everything is different. The door opens, Zanne comes into the bathroom, stands next to her. Bea is crying hard now.

"Why?" Zanne asks. "I should be," and begins to. They are locked into an embrace, not touching, the endless tunnel of their faces coining themselves in the mirrors.

"I didn't even get nauseated," Zanne says in the cab the next day.

Later, Bea brings Zanne warm milk and buttered toast and a banana. "Gerber's," she says.

"Ohhhh, owwww," Zanne says. "You should be a doctor, you just cut so well."

"You'll feel better tomorrow," Bea tells her.

"Or a nurse," says Zanne.

Bea holds her, rocks her. "Or the day after," she says.

She does, four days after. "I love you," Bea tells her in the bus station, the words coming unintended. Zanne looks at her as if she can barely understand. They leave Chicago, broke, a terrible feeling of loss. "Where did you get the money?" Bea asks.

"For it? The Divino Italiano. The bastard! Why?"

"I wanted to really hate him," Bea says.

Now Bea has missed two weeks of class. Thinking about it makes her stomach hurt again. Her roommate's boyfriend has moved into her bed. "He doesn't have anyplace to sleep," her roommate tells her. Bea thinks to herself she should go home, face the music of her father's wasted money. Her Italian teacher, Professor Alberti, breaks into crocodile tears when she tells him she is dropping out of school. Bea looks at him and thinks this is the race; Dante, Michelangelo, the Red Brigade, Umberto? What would the little tyke have been? Frank Sinatra? Pope? "The people who invented life," the professor says, "ice cream, spaghetti. Well, they didn't invent them, actually," he told her (the price of a semester), "but they made them good."

Zanne got over the postpartum (interrupted) depression; Umberto, almost as a passing score for a test he'd imposed on Zanne, proposed. "Tell him you'll let him know," Bea advises her when she phones.

"Let him know? He's on his knees."

"You probably shouldn't have called me then," Bea tells her and hangs up.

Bea calls her other sister, Pat, asks her what God, according to her minister husband, would say about this.

"I'll put him on." He is tall, thin with gold wire-rimmed spectacles, always on the verge of tears or laughter though he has never done either in front of Bea.

"Marry him," he says.

"Not me," Bea tells him. "Zanne."

"Forgive, forget. Marry. Stay married. Reproduce."

"Did you find a church?" Bea asks.

"I'm working in a music store. Bach and God, Pat and me, the baby. You have to learn to be happy, the way you learn anything else."

Bea gets a job at the Photo Bug, gives half her salary to her parents to help pay back her tuition. In the Bug she learns about exposures and apertures. *Camera* is the Italian word for room. "That means something. I am in a larger room. Dante could explain," she thinks.

"I am going back to college," she tells herself, begins the long and arduous trek to the inside of her father's head where the money and the permission are kept. When, for no reason other than that of being unreasonable, Bobby Corbett, her ideal, calls and asks for a date she considers the difference between a dream come true and a dream, aches from saying no. She counts the months, saves her other half from the Bug, kisses Zanne when she says *sì, sì*, to Umberto. He kisses her. Her parents kiss him. He kisses them. They kiss Zanne. Zanne kisses Bea, Pat, the baby, who have come for the event. Bea watches them, thinks of love, love with reservations, as it always appears to be given. "I love you," as long as you keep your body from doing something untoward. You can break your heart the way you break your leg, but it's between you and your doctor. Bea thinks of the Italian word for kisses. *Baci*. She wishes she could remember the word for mistakes. *Baci* also means meringues, the sweet clouds of eggwhites and sugar they have for dessert on special occasions. The same words can mean so many different things, she thinks with surprise. "Baby" meant something terrible to Zanne and Umberto, something wonderful for another couple. You had to learn the right word. If you didn't the word would come to life, get you around the neck, haunt you, strangle. Totally. "Totally," for example. She hated the word. "The room was *totally* dark." "She had a *total* relapse." Then the word came to life. "She was *totally* dead." And suddenly there was a girl who wasn't. The girl's parents had to go to court to have a judge and jury and panel of experts decide whether she was dead. *Totally* dead. Something in between? If the word existed for a state of being that would make death worse than it was, it could happen to her. The violence of education began to strike her. She wasn't sure finding out was for her. Life in the Bug began to seem safer and safer.

Walking, Walking

"Sleep," Rosa said. "If I don't get sleep."

Not sleeping, her son David had told her when he worked at the hospital, would make you go crazier than anything, and the competition, he said, was pretty stiff. He had been dead these two years and she saw him now, walking, walking.

"He can't sleep," she said, explaining to herself there was no such thing as ghosts, "I can't sleep."

She saw him perilously close to some edge. The world? Or their flat neighborhood spread like a poor supper on a table above the town. Then saw him veering away from the edge, stiffly sober as he never had been in life, canny when once he had been foolish and vulnerable. He was tired, and she had tried to transfer some of his tiredness to herself by worrying, a burden added to the overwhelming fatigue she already felt from not sleeping. But tired as he must've been, he kept on walking, and she felt she had to keep up her vigil with him.

Rosa's head, wrapped in a napkin, was ball-like so that coming at her from the side it seemed you might be seeing her from the front. The head looked something like a frog's, the eyes large, the mouth rounding inward. Not a real frog, an obsidian or carnelian frog; some rare hard stone.

She had seen Little David laid out in the tuxedo they had told her the burial insurance didn't cover and she had had to pay extra for. She had paid that $2.98 a week virtually forever, since she was eighteen, fifty some-odd years ago. For herself. How could she have known she'd outlive him? The insurance people had argued the policy wasn't transferable, but it was, finally, if she made up the difference of the better box and went on paying the $2.98, now upped to $4.98; and she had wished more—David's death, his little body—could've been transferable too so that she would've been lying there surrounded by the cool peach of pink gladiolas and he would've been in her place, puzzled, sleepless, alone, but alive. Alive, anything might happen: dead, nothing would. Except for this which she couldn't figure out, her seeing him, his seeming to want to explain something.

She had walked by the casket a thousand times. She had thought of his saying one day about a friend of hers who had died and worse than died, been pursued, by pain, by people who wanted her to pay money she didn't have, that the friend had gone "where nobody could touch her."

"And where's that?" Rosa had asked.

He had seemed embarrassed. Then he'd said, turning around, "Religion's ignorant. You learn that in nursing school. What makes people sick or well isn't faith, hope, or charity!"

What was odd about what he had said was that the same things that made you well made you sick. After a lifetime she wasn't sure about religion, only that she took any help she could get, and that religion went beyond her idea of peace as lying in a satin-lined box surrounded by heavy-smelling flowers. It was useful, she thought, like the friend she had invented to keep from going crazy.

"I see him!" she exclaimed to the woman, her creation, a reasonable, straight-haired creature who spoke about "her people" and was in politics, as invisible as Little David though Rosa saw her, light-skinned, smooth-faced, as falsely soothing as cornbread with sugar in it.

"Where?" the woman demanded, Rosa changing her voice. "Not in your dreams if you ain't sleeping. Not around here because everything you see in this house I see! His room, your room, this room!"

This room was the main room, kitchen, living room, dressing room, because of the stove. Rosa was proud of the house, its working, the pump in the sink that froze up and only she could get going, the stove she got red hot even with wet wood, the unwired, unplumbed house behind the Seven-Eleven that was such a surviving oddity the historical society had asked to come in, once, to see it and make a tape-recording of "what she remembered." Rosa said she couldn't remember.

"I was forty-two when I got him," Rosa said to the imaginary companion, the woman she deemed childless in her imagination, and for whom she remembered everything. "I remember the night—clean—as if it was tonight! He in me a year, no nine months." The woman nodded agreeably as if such biological inaccuracies were part of their suffering.

"A year! They say, 'Rosa, you stick out any more they can't get to you to deliver that baby!' You ever notice how mens know everything about having babies?" The smooth-faced woman chuckled softly. "Experience don't count for nothing in this place. And he won't come and he won't come. They say he dead in me. You know what that is? They have to deliver it the same way they deliver a live baby. You sitting there waiting a year and they got to reach way up inside you and haul out a itty-bitty corpse."

The woman made a sour face and said, as if the potential horrors of childbirth were well dispelled by the fact, "But David's alive!"

"They turn over and over in you," Rosa said. "He's turning over in me now." She looked up at the door to indicate Little David was walking across the porch.

"Watch out!" she yelled. "You fall into them rotten boards I can't get you!"

"You'd get him no matter where he fell," the woman said sympathetically.

And Rosa had, when he'd fallen into easy ways, drinking the health of tomorrow before the evil of today was taken care of, being led by loose friends, had sworn she'd go with him to the end, bitter only because she could see it was an end and she couldn't stop it being one. They could still have been going on, mother and son, worrying about such minor difficulties as whether she was making a mama's boy of him at thirty. She asked herself whether—if she had let him fall then, into a shallow hole—she might've saved him from the worse one he was walking around in now.

A raspy-tongued cat, she had scrubbed him from a child, going over his groin, pushing the washcloth hard as steelwool against a pot, seeing him growing up, the moment of becoming a man, bending him over the hide-bottomed ladderback chair in front of the stove. Fourteen, he had said, "No, I'm too big." Rosa thought now, wrong not to let him go; she had confused his small size with his maturity, but she should've looked inside his head: he was independent there. He died the same small size. She had picked up the iron she pressed shirts with and heated on the stove when he said no more scrubbing, had come across his face, missing—she told herself years since— on purpose, hitting his shoulder with the glancing blow that caused him to lean to the left the rest of his life, a glancing blow because the iron was so heavy she could not manage it once it had left the power of her hand, the power that made his shirts dazzling.

David had got his job at the hospital, Rosa knew, on the strength of the dazzling shirts she had ironed for him and his willingness to wash and change incontinent patients. She had beamed when the head nurse told her, "We got plenty nuclear-medical specialists and space doctors out here and *one* common laborer: *Him*, I trade you five nuclear medical specialists for one *him*!"

Rosa could've blamed everything on Little David's father but she didn't know him past being glad he had gone. He had loved her for periods of quarter-hours. He had had no thought for time beyond those periods and she had had thoughts for nothing else. Little David had been half him. But he hadn't stopped at half a bottle. The other half must've been her. There was some desire she had passed on to him that kept him thirsty then, walking now.

The trouble with Little David was he couldn't amuse himself. He had had the good job driving Dr. Mulherin. One-legged Dr. Mulherin delivered every baby in town. His name was legion, almost as legion as Washington. And while Dr. Mulherin was delivering, Little David was nipping.

WALKING, WALKING

When the county replaced Dr. Mulherin and his midwives with its own hospital (and baby deaths shot up, the old doctor said) he had his bird collections to occupy him. David, at twenty-one, was too shaky to climb trees and bring down eggs from the nests. "I'd go myself but for the leg," Dr. Mulherin said, and hired a younger, soberer, agile boy. Dr. Mulherin got David into practical-nursing classes. He was quick, he understood the courses. But between classes. In the bathroom? Standing outside the hospital in the alley on fine days? Rosa couldn't teach him to amuse himself because she couldn't understand what spare time was herself.

Rosa lay down, closed her eyes, and was wide awake. The others—how was it a person could be completely alone, lose her husband, her son, parents, all sisters, one brother, and still have relatives?—came and went, saying she was crazy, or asking to see him, agreeing, sharing the vision. "Yes! I see him! There!" "In a white robe? The peace on his face? Yes!"

The relatives explained it was perfectly normal, or had they said perfectly natural? They said it was God's footprint on her brain, that it—did they mean him?—would go away. With time. Time! There was no such thing. You had only to be in a hurry to learn that.

Rosa thought and thought—it was not normal. Or natural either. Something was causing Little David to pad about. Wearing the tuxedo.

That meant he had come straight on from the funeral instead of going anywhere else first, home or purgatory, and the tuxedo itself was unnatural, a flimsy sort of facade like a building in a ghost town or the starched bibs that Chaplin used to wear in movies. What a church that Chaplin must've run, she thought. In heaven since it seemed unlikely she would ever get to California, she would like to visit that man's church, hear him preach, see the bib pop off from the trouser button they didn't even put on new pants now and slap him in the face. Little David's tuxedo was like that. Only it had no pants, just

sort of a black apron that went to his knees. No back. For what
they charged her, she thought, it should have had a train. An-
gels to hold it up. His poor little legs! The walking, walking,
pushing against the sleazy black apron. The little clip-on bow
tie. He needed a real one, a satin butterfly she would tie as
lightly as the ribbon around his baby neck she had bowed the
day of his baptism.

Her age, she was afraid, was closing in on her. She had to get
him to bed or to sleep before she went. Or, dead too, there
would be two of them. Moving around an inch or two above
the ground, like a hydrofoil she'd seen, floating on air above
the water unable to get themselves down.

The letter that came was almost a note from him. He leaned
toward her across the distance, motioning her to read it as she
saw on the envelope titles and styles ("Mrs." her husband's
names) she had not worn for so long she wondered who they
were talking to. "Madame." Dear Madame: They were going to
dig up his grave. With her permission. They were going to dig
up the whole cemetery. It was harder, they hinted, to get permission from the dead than the living and so they would ap-
preciate cooperation. "They bought a stamp to tell you that?"
the woman said, reading over her shoulder.

"Eminent domain," the letter stated, "to connect a vital ac-
cess to another." "'They' would dig to China if you let them,"
the woman murmured. "Wake my people up from their only
rest!" Rosa thought she was going to sing a hymn.

The highway was coming. They would pay for the exhumation. They had the permission of the state. The county coroner.
The coroner's physician would be in attendance. There was a
hearing scheduled. She could attend with her lawyer or other
"representative." Rosa did not understand how that could be—
the letter was *from* a representative.

She held the letter up to the light. It seemed almost to take
on the shape of David's face, losing its square edges, the paper

matching, equaling the face, his face paler and paler next to it in the distance, his body thinner and thinner like winter sun through the clouds. He seemed to grow toward her, flatter and flatter, to fix her with his stare.

The second letter—Little David had come very close this time—so close she thought she could grab him and "put him down"—she used to say that for putting him to bed when he was a baby—but when she reached, her hands went through air. She had not chosen to attend the hearing, it said, or even to send her "representative"; they understood this as consent. The exhumation would take place "on or about" December twenty-first at an hour she couldn't somehow remember.

It was the shortest day of the year. Rosa was grateful for that.

David, half naked, the cold cracking his poor skin, the very light skin that anything, even a mosquito bite, scarred, his tiny butt that never quite filled out his underwear pants, exposed to the gaping people digging up his grave, would have less time in the merciless winter light that never warmed.

She dressed carefully. Out the front door, the intense winter sun blinding her, she realized she was wearing the black dress she had worn to his funeral. The light-skinned woman smiled: her perfect teeth, Rosa saw in the dazzling light, were not her own. The minted scent of properly soaked dentures wafted past her nose. She saw David's nostrils flare. He was leading them.

At the street he pointed to her shoe that was untied. She bent over to tie it and just as she tightened the knot, lost her balance, the wind spanking her, and she sat down hard on the cold pavement. She had not put on underwear believing somehow he might try to get back inside her. That the year he had spent there had not been enough and she must present no hindrance to his journey back.

He threw up his arms in front of her, closer to her than he had ever been, even in life. The weariness in his face gave way to glee. He mouthed the words, "You see?" She nodded to him, as unable to understand his meanness as his wanting to be separate from her in life, her dreams for him. Maybe, she thought hoping, he had learned to amuse himself. In life he had been sweet, he had been obedient, but he didn't want to be part. He had had the extra job when he was able, to try to earn money for the refrigerator they told him couldn't be plugged into the house. He had tried to help, but he didn't want to be *with* her or anybody else. He liked the company of drinking, *doing* it as much as the taste of wine itself. When he had become visible after death, she knew there would be plenty of company for him out there, people who couldn't rest, things like drinking and girling that liked to get the best of you, forces, powers that made you drop things and gave the falling things the anger they would have had had they been thrown. A biscuit dropped from the table could break your foot if it wanted to, it gained such momentum from somewhere. Things could hurt you hard as people; stub your toe, cut you, worry you crazy.

Rosa thought the woman with her should've offered her comfort, her arm or some shortcut to the cemetery. The sidewalk was overgrown. Everyone who passed this way had cars now. Children went to school on the bus.

Rosa was not used to walking long stretches anymore. She felt dizzy. The sun burned her eyes. She wished she'd worn a broad-brim hat. She even wished for a moment he would go away, leave her to ordinary grief. She'd go back to her cold bed and lie down; now she felt she could sleep. Maybe she could pity him better when she woke up. But the woman took on a superior look that said, We must go on. Rosa could hear some spiritual proclaiming strength in suffering.

At the cemetery, Rosa's presence had not been needed to begin. The backhoe had already dug up graves, the truck was loaded with muddy caskets. Over Little David's grave—she knew it by the cedar tree, almost red now from the winter cold—the arm of a derrick, raised like the hand of a blessing, held a dangling empty concrete rectangle, coffinless, Little Davidless. There was no bottom, no top to the vault which the funeral home man had said was permanent. She approached the grave. A man in waders, startlingly close, peered up at her from the mud in the hole. For a moment she thought the man was trying to take David's place. The mud seemed like quicksand, and the man shifted his weight, left foot, right foot. He must've been cold too, in the grave with mud and ice water around his feet.

Two men came toward her. Yes, it was her grave, her son's. No, she saw nothing in it, either. It had been, she told them, *solid bronze.* It would last, the funeral home had said, forever. She had the written guarantee. Not a handle, the men told her, a hinge, or a screw had been found. There'd be something, they said. It might be rusty, but there'd be something. Wasn't it just two years? Two years wouldn't destroy everything. "I could argue that," her friend, stepping around the excavations, said. Across what was now a field, the cedars and yews having been largely bulldozed, she saw David, his teeth exposed, Rosa couldn't tell, in a grimace or a smile.

They drove her, which was a relief, warm, in their car, to an office in the courthouse and explained and asked questions about who buried David and whether she had put any gold or silver in the box, things like jewelry or a watch, or "money," they said, winking at each other, "for the trip." Then they drove her to the medical school where a young woman who seemed frightened of Rosa and wouldn't look her straight in the eye told them *their* bodies came from the state asylum or she (it was part of her job) asked for the bodies from the relatives of indigents who wanted to avoid the final payment of a funeral. They would never buy a body from "a questionable source." She had her records, they could look at them. They turned then to Rosa. Had *she*? What did they take her for? They hadn't meant that, they said. Had only turned to ask her if she had an idea. What did they do with the cadavers, they asked the young woman, when the medical students were finished? The young woman had an answer though Rosa's friend who had squeezed into the car with them looked skeptical, as if her people were being exploited. The sanitation department came, the girl said she alerted them, they came especially, nothing else in the truck, no garbage, she put it, and they carried the remains off to the city incinerator.

The path, Rosa thought, then led to the funeral home. The owner stood on the porch defending himself, the high columns that had been sewer pipes and had no relation to the rest of the building except for being painted white rising behind him.

Rosa saw the undertaker listen to her, the men. Representatives from the district attorney's office he had dealt with before, she imagined, even contributed to. But her eyes didn't blink.

"You said it was solid bronze," she said, fairly quietly.

"Solidbronz!" he told her. "A registered trademark! Nothing lasts forever." With his luck today, he thought, the same box was sitting in the salesroom waiting like some girl at a dance, to be chosen, and this woman—and he knew her—was the sort to have scratched her initials in the side when she knelt, wailing by the bier of her son, two years ago, the sort to run her hands under the box and feel the little trap door that allowed the frail body to exit the strong box. Where? He'd forgotten. It was foolish, wasn't it, he thought, almost asking her, she seemed so reasonable, to waste a three thousand dollar box? When it was as good as new? So foolish to give in to wet ground when wet eyes had to dry and go home. Unchristian! Where your treasure lies so also lies your heart! Leave it in the ground?

One of the men, he thought, to frighten him, recited another case, said something about greed: "They resold the shrouds twice! Thirty cents each. Piece of sheet!" The man from the DA's office looked at him as though he were recounting a parable from the Bible, its weight past the necessity of explanation. There was a reason the man had mentioned money. He was running for office on this visit. The funeral home man grasped the equation. He turned to Rosa. She was so realistic, what people used to call "wise," when you could afford to be poor, before water bills and light bills could change your life.

She understood people making money. But this was supposed to be a place of necessary grief. You came here in your last hour, not to God. Nothing was free; everybody knew that, but even God listened a moment for the money you paid. The undertaker and the DA man seemed to be splitting apart here, the DA more sympathetic. David, pale as the false columns outside that held up the roof, stood square behind the undertaker. Odd, Rosa thought, her son would've sided with the man who'd cheated her. Paying the money, she thought, for the coffin, was like saying a prayer, a required ritual; results anybody's guess; like a guarantee, a word that no longer obtained. The man's gypping her had turned back on him. David wasn't in the box. David had got out. David had broken his bonds, David was loose. He could improve now. The figure, walking alone, that had worried her now pleased her, slowly, like the heat in the car which, after the long walk in the cold, had seeped sweetly, complete, around her swollen ankles and knees, soothed them, and made the motion and comfort of the body possible and infinite. Jesus had let that woman wash his feet with her hair and oil him up good. Little David was moving, lifting. She had seen his pitiful little backside and shivered for him. He had washed the backsides of the sick and dying when nobody else would and carried out the buckets. Not everybody saw that side in people, she thought, some just saw the tuxedo side. Those people would do the same thing to live people this funeral home man had done to the dead, dress them up, box them, throw them away. She knew David now couldn't blame her for anything. He'd have been better off if he'd let her follow him the way she scrubbed him in life.

Suddenly, she turned, asked the man if he saw David. The quick consummation in the undertaker's eyes, his thinking this craziness would go against her, that they would excuse him because of her, thrilled her with its connivance. Like her relatives, the man caught the tone.

"Yes!" he fairly shouted. "I see him! Crowned!" and his eyes, yellowish and bulging, rolled back in his head so the people from the DA's office could see. They were smart enough to give no sign; Rosa knew they were thinking about elections; she was only one vote; the undertaker was a precinct power.

Still the men paused, staring at her, her strangeness, her virtue in letting go. They saw that the knowledge the man had cheated her seemed to please her as much as any damages might.

"David's in the sky," she said, quietly satisfied.

"Escaped," the undertaker whispered under his breath.

The men might smile at each other later, over a drink, though now they were unable to, staring at this minor revelation that was somehow disturbing. They kept looking at Rosa, looking for a way to understand her without giving her any credit, to find themselves back on the concrete of their own beliefs and certainties. She returned the stares, blinkless, forcing upon them the enigma of differences. There was no noise in the room. Rosa's steady eyes grew, never leaving the men. They looked uneasily at the ring of caskets around the room, the choices, the dull tones of silver, bronze, gold, the thin metal— no more than foil—covering the wood—or plastic?—boxes. It was as though they could hear something through the silence: Rosa's anguish. Flesh whining. Damned of earth, damned of air. But staring at Rosa they knew they could hear nothing.

Home, Rosa felt she could sleep. She took off her dress slowly, squinted hard at the image of David, his feet thick and crusty from years of going barefoot, the tuxedo front no more than a black veil covering his nakedness now. The edges of his hands and feet, like a leper's, began to blanch and fade.

The light-skinned friend glanced at her with pity and contempt—a woman whose grasp had exceeded her reach—and moved into the light surrounding the softening form of David. Rosa made one more desperate lunge for him. Her hands came back wet. Everything she could remember was wet: the man standing in the grave with his feet in water; the little drops that would find the leaks in the roof above her and trickle in, traveling halfway across the house along a beam to find an opening, water, like civilization, always seeking the lowest level. It was raining outside, bright slashes that would turn to ice before dark.

Rosa smoothed the clean, cold sheets. The force of her weariness pressed down on her. She tried to find the mind that had found David, known he was not where she had buried him, but there was only a feeling of loss, like static from the radio during a storm. Those people today had not been able to count the dead much less the living. She thought of souls, numberless souls, still wandering around in the void. She wished she could follow each of them the way she had David. Through her flickering eyelids she saw less and less of him until there were only bright bits fighting against the rain. Even as he dissolved the lilt of his body where she had struck him stayed and she felt the iron in her hand, lighter than her sleep.

The Water Cure

Art has finally got the best of Mrs. Ionides. "The Rape of Europe" hangs down so far from the ceiling in her painting-and-sculpture-cluttered apartment it covers half her bedroom door. Passing in or out of her room, she has to duck, something she forgets to do at 2 A.M. when the cat, Titian, deposits a pair of damp, gasping chimney swifts on her bed and she runs into the kitchen for some newspapers to wrap the poor sooty things in. Where her head hits the canvas, part of the bull where the painting's stretcher is worm-riddled and weak comes away and sticks to her cold-creamed forehead. The maid, Ursula, superstitious to begin with and always afraid of the punishment Mrs. Ionides owes her for sleeping with the late Mr. Ionides, sees the grinning bull pasted on top of the naked figure and runs into the street crossing herself and screaming for the police.

"Ursie! Ursie!" Mrs. Ionides, half-dressed, calls, "Not a real bull! Ha! Just me!"

In the Italian town of Chioggia where Minerva Ionides lives across the lagoon from Venice, the boats, *bragozzi*, motorized now but still equipped with saint-painted sails for luck, remind her of how her husband made his small, largely squandered on paintings, fortune. His boats, his "collection"—put in quotation marks by a young man whose fare Minnie had to pay out from London to evaluate the pictures as "nothing but canvas"—his being Greek made him think he was Onassis or Niarchos.

Most of the fish the boats netted comes frozen now from Iceland or South America. Whatever else they used to haul—oil or gas—will be brought overland by pipe from Russia. The villa where her husband spread out his collection has been confiscated by the state as a home for mental patients: Minnie and Ursula have moved into this small apartment. Minnie protested the takeover, but in truth she was happy; the roof leaked, no one would work in the yard, the noisy furnace nurtured her insomnia. But she can't part with anything, especially Ursula, who regards herself as the propitiation for Mr. Ionides's sins. When Minnie says the word "sins" it sounds obsolescent, vast and unuseful like the extra bedrooms in the villa she was glad to be rid of.

Her husband's infidelity still afflicts her, more so because, dead, he can never set it right and she has to bear the burden of his past, the guilt she feels he would assume alive, her age, his exuberant heart tamed by a bypass, or a pacemaker.

In the tiny apartment Ursula sleeps in the kitchen, but Minnie can't do without her. Once Ursula timidly suggested, "If you moved that out"—pointing to a plaster cast of the Laocoön (the movers had had to cut out the window to get it in) . . . Smash wine glasses on her husband's tomb, it sounded like to Minnie.

Minnie found her at the police station—Oh, she knew it wasn't a real bull!

Minnie admonishes her: "If it had been, you'd leave me alone with it?"

"I went for help!" Ursula says, tearfully.

The young *poliziotto* stares at Ursula, then at the half-dressed Mrs. Ionides. He has the limited contrition of a waiter who can't remember who's ordered what and won't admit it but finds the dishes too hot to hold.

"Birds in the chimney!" Minnie explains to him, his brown eyes as strong as breakfast coffee. Ursula sobs, grasps the police desk; she has a way of crying that makes her chest shake, showing off the pretty roundness of her bosom.

Years before, Mr. Ionides guaranteed the girl's chastity—the easiest thing in the world to do—to Ursula's mother, who saw the position as a great opportunity. He might tire of his wife. Away from Greece where they lived lay the world. The threatened alternative for Ursula was the convent.

The policeman's thick shining hair lifts slightly in the wind from the open door. Minnie wants to touch; her hand shoots out, tugs through the smooth hair, lingering before finding, "Ha! A mosquito!" He follows her hand to see, but Minnie has already flicked the imaginary insect away.

Her arm around Ursula's waist, she leads her back to the apartment where she experiences the indignity of waiting on her maid, slightly hysterical, heating milk, putting her in her own bed while she makes up the cot in the kitchen for herself. Ursula tells her she is coming down with a cold. "Water, water!" Minnie says. "Drink plenty water; drown yourself!"

Trying to sleep, Ursula thinks Mrs. Ionides's keeping her from men is part of her punishment for having shared Mr. Ionides's bed. Did she think there had been a choice? Did she imagine there had been any pleasure?

Minerva Ionides wakes up half an hour later to the sound of the doorbell. Her bathrobe is in her bedroom. She can't find her wrapper, puts on her rings, wraps the kitchen tablecloth around her slightly overweight body, goes downstairs very carefully. The young *poliziotto* stands on the stone stoop. Minnie clutches the tablecloth tight around her body. He does not look at her, but past her, up the stairs, his eyes going around corners, through doors, to the form of the girl asleep beneath *her* sheets, coarse linen, the tatting on the edges stiff and hard. He does not say anything. Minnie is determined she will not speak first. She shivers in the air. He takes out a report and hands it to her, his eyes never leaving upstairs. She holds it in her ringed fingers, sees the report, says nothing.

"An excuse to see her!" she says, thinking her voice will intimidate him or wake her.

"What is all that stuff?" he asks, holding the door and pointing to the steps behind her lined with demolished palazzo fragments. A narrow path with numerous infringements allows a limited flow of traffic up and down. The walls are thick with baroque frames, too small or too large for pictures that hang underneath, around, or on top of them.

"Your past!" she says. "The past I kept for you!" She slams

the door. She thinks since her husband's death, these things have become her substance, the respectability of a past with which she can challenge his lover. Carefully threading her way up the stairs through ogival arch tops and broken balusters, she hears her starched sheets scratching Ursula's young body. She peers in to see her stretching, a live version of one of numerous nudes languorously staring down from the walls, from pictures leaning on pictures, more pictures propped against a terra-cotta Venus on which Ursula has hung her brassiere and panties.

Minnie looks at the sheets. "What did you do? Bivouac?"

The cat emerges, showing pride of place over person, his face stuck with the chimney swift's feathers.

"Go back to sleep," Minnie says to Ursula, making sure she is awake.

Restless, Minnie decides to get rid of something. She staggers under a gigantic Sansovino frame, rickety but still tainted with grandeur, and starts down the stairs. She imagines herself the portrait in the empty frame, some Renaissance patron of the arts. She holds her head, trying to show off her profile for the artist, too high, unbalancing her wobbly figure. A third of the way down, the frame wire catches on a projecting piece of stone. The frame begins to come apart: she cannot let go, continues her descent while the frame tries to remain behind. She senses each misstep as Galileo's notion of attractions, pulling her disastrously to the bottom, the Renaissance, civilization's highest achievement, brought down by nature's basest instinct, gravity. A nail from the frame lifts a jagged fold of skin in the shape of a Z across her forehead. She hits the bottom with a heavy thud, thinking, "I'm still alive," only to have her head, thrown back during the descent, come forward to contest her belief—bang!—against the mail slot.

"I'm all right!" she cries after a moment to reassure Ursula, who hears nothing. Then Minnie sees the blood, so much that she wonders whether it is paint somehow melting from the pictures.

"Help!" she calls out, in English for emphasis.

Ursula sleeps. On the floor, Minnie listens to herself, hears her pulse, violent and loud. She picks up the largest remnant of the frame and starts back up the stairs thinking it is foolish to sell her husband's possessions because they are hers now. "They won't bring any money," she says wondering if she is delirious.

At the top, surprised she has made it, she calls out again. Ursula thinks it is time for breakfast, wanders out into the hall, yawning. She sees Minnie, stares, frozen in a silent scream.

"Get some towels!" Minnie orders.

Ursula's mouth drops open again. "Blood?" she asks.

"Sauce Bolognese," Minnie says, goes into the bathroom, bends over the tub searching out her oldest towels in the cabinet. Blood rains from her head into the bath. Ursula is still in the hall, paralyzed. "I'm bliding! Get your police!"

Minnie waits what seems forever before she hears the door downstairs pushed against a timid knock, then the bell.

"Stupid!" she thinks. "Forget the key!"

A blood-soaked towel around her head, Minnie traces her fallen footsteps, in each step a lively fear she will repeat her dive, opens the door, faints into the young *poliziotto*'s arms, drenching him.

When she comes to in the doctor's office, he asks her, "What's your lucky number?"

She says, "Thirteen."

"Thirteen stitches? Signora! Lucky! A centimeter more and Pfft! No eye!"

She groans with each stitch. "How much?"

"Less if you don't make the racket!" the doctor says. "You want something for pain?"

"You're not enough?"

"Included in the bill."

"Any less if you don't give it?"

The doctor looks at her, sewn and bandaged. "Becoming," he says.

Minnie looks in the mirror. "More 'becoming' if it hid more," she says, grateful her lined forehead will be smoothed, out of sight. She examines the statement. "An old woman! A widow! I bring you a penting instead."

"*I* bring the painting!" Ursula says, envisioning Minnie, art laden, on the way down again.

"Wounds on the head heal very quickly," the doctor says to Ursula as if warning her to expect sanity or worse from her mistress.

Ursula delivers the painting the next day, her policeman on the other end, a note inserted into a rent in the canvas with Minnie's, "Very easy repaired," on it. The doctor keeps the painting and the following day his bill, double, arrives with *per favore* underlined in red.

Minnie stays in bed three days. Ursula massages her neck, her sore shoulders, dusts the pictures.

"You're a good girl, Ursie!" Minnie says. "I do something for you?"

Ursula has asked to be taken to the Redentore to see the relics of her patron saint. The two women have started out several times but always wind up in an art gallery where Minnie buys or talks about another picture. In her loneliness and reduced circumstances the gallery owners have been her only friends. They discuss her collection, ask her about the past, its tastes and discernments, as though she were part of art history. She winces at how like her dead husband she has become: *Mrs.* Niarchos, she thinks.

Thursday, three days after the fall, the day before the stitches are to come out, Minnie and Ursula set out for the church. Minnie wants to show off her bandage; she imagines the visitors to the city who see her will think she is a true Venetian, shaky, enduring, like the fragments on her stairs, beautiful because they were once perfect.

"Nobody!" she cries over the motor of the *vaporetto*, "nobody could have a *crise nerveuse* here!" The two women are jammed and rejammed into the boat.

"Nerves?" Ursula asks, by now knowing most of Minnie's foreign phrases.

"A nervous breakdown! All this water, these people fondling you, looking into your mouth. You don't even have to say ahhhh! They don't even have bank robberies here—they don't have nerves!"

"No escape!" Ursula says. "No getaway cars." Two young men pressed against her look into her open mouth like dentists ferreting out cavities. Minnie notices she is held differently from the way her maid is held by the other passengers: they enfold Ursula, men or women, but they grip her tightly, as if she is fried fish they don't want to get their hands greasy on. She blames their reticence on her bandaging.

She feels wildly happy as they get down in the Riva degli Schiavone. Minnie imagines scenographic Venice here, another painting in her collection. Wind from the Adriatic ruffles the waves, lifting cabbages, pink and green melon rinds like moons and suns in the pale blue water. Ursula laughs at the spray that whips across the landing stage, cooling her bare legs.

"You know, Signora? Your water cure? You say I should drink bucket and bucket? I laugh! But I have the cold and I drink, drink! In one day, one day, all well!" She is very serious. "Don't buy no more painting!"

The remonstrance, Minnie thinks, is a message from her dead husband. He has left his messages with Ursula, not with her, his spokesman in death and in what followed, the maze of sorrow and relief and loneliness.

Minnie will not give Ursula household money for extra bread and butter. They have not had meat for six weeks. "You don't want to get fet!" she always says when Ursula asks for more money for groceries. "You see what's happened to me."

But Minnie is determined she will not spoil the outing; she is happy to be alive with both her eyes.

"Figs!" she says. "We just want to buy a few figs. Then we go to Redentore."

They emerge into the small *campo* on the other side of the

Rialto. The light from the paved square with its failure of plumb where the larch pilings have settled over the centuries is almost human in its crooked determination. She imagines the paintings her husband, and now she, couldn't stop buying were an attempt to fix this scene into a small, purchasable, ownable form, ideal, as the gallery owners constantly tell her, "for small apartments."

The fruit vendor is sitting on the well head. She tries to remember who—Napoleon?—closed the wells and put in the central water system. As usual he cannot remember her though she has bought figs from him for years. The word is perilously close to the Italian word for the female genitalia. A favorite sport among waiters in expensive restaurants and hotels in the city is to pretend not to understand what is being ordered until the foreigner is shouting the word at top-lung, pronunciation astray in volume and frustration, and people are turning around to see why a table of tourists is bellowing an obscenity loud enough to make the chandeliers tinkle.

Minnie touches the green ones, from Ischia, the black and purple ones from Sicily, Capri. Her hand moves suggestively. He waves it away, puts the fruit into a pressed paper sack, as many overripe ones as good. When she complains, he says, "They don't ripen after they're picked."

"Why do you pick them then if they're not ripe?" He ignores her, adds 300 lire to the bill, says he will not be back next year.

"But you said that last year!" Minnie tells him.

"*Sì, sì,* every year!"

Minnie's feet, as if they were the false promises of the fruit vendor, lead her through passages and over marble bridges that come, she tries to believe without intent, to the picture sellers' quarter. Most of the shops are no more than single rooms, furnished with a gilt chair, a table, a dusky mirror that makes all faces look young, part of the carnival past. But the rooms are miraculously connected to supply systems that in moments can produce any variation, color, character, scene, or size in a painting to fit different decorating schemes, different tastes. "The Japanese of Europe," Minnie thinks, as Ursula tries to drag her away. She wonders who peoples this vast cottage industry, knows only that she is their reason for being. She stares into a shop. Her feet hurt. The dealer glances up, recognizes his prey, and, reading her mind, smiles, pointing to the gilded chair.

Ursula grabs her arm. "No!" But Minnie is already inside, tottering to the gold chair.

The dealer offers lemon squash, pushes forward a little needlework footstool.

"But where will I put it?" she says laughingly at herself over a little panel she is almost persuaded to buy.

"Put it back!" Ursula whispers.

"It's not real," the dealer says, qualifying his remark when he sees Minnie has not guessed, "I mean, not old. Scenes with the Bucintoro are so rare!"

"A lovely custom," Minnie says admiring the gilded barge, the Doge on the prow casting a golden ring into the water, "one I've often thought should be revived. 'We marry thee, oh sea!'"

The dealer smiles, thinking she must not know Napoleon burned the ceremonial barge. "It's reduced," he says, offering the bargain, thinking he has others.

Ursula waves no wildly behind the man's back, wiggles her fingers in horns on his head. Minnie remembers coming home one night from church and finding Ursula draped with damask altar cloths, her husband's face buried in her young breasts. The walnut cupids carved on their bedstead seemed to smirk. The same altar hangings stuff her closet now, wrinkling her dresses. Minnie says, "I'll take it."

They have a pimento and anchovy sandwich on the Zattere. Minnie insists on removing the little painted panel from its wrapping to look at it. She imagines the tourists eating next to her think she is returning to one of the glimmering white yachts anchored across the canal at San Giorgio Maggiore, that she has bought a masterpiece as casually as they have purchased postcards. She orders Ursula, a living easel, to hold the picture different ways to catch the light, but high winds whip clouds across the sun and lift Ursula's skirt, embarrassing her because she is not wearing a slip.

"Half a washing machine!" she says very low to Minnie. "We could have bought half a washing machine!"

"A quarter, maybe," Minnie says. "When we're dead and gone who'll remember our laundry?"

Oddly, no one is waiting for the boat. Minnie thinks, "How fortunate," climbs in with Ursula. The pilot looks puzzled.

"You live in the Giudecca?" he asks.

It was, when the Ionides first came to Venice, a poor quarter. Minnie draws herself up to say "Indeed not!" but the pilot anticipates her.

"It's no disgrace. You may not get back!"

The waves are rising. Tankers leave an oily wake high as a wall that threatens to swamp them. She thinks the man means the weather. "This little footpath!" she snorts. "I'm a sailor's wife! A Greek!" The man stares, cross-eyed, at the bandage on her head.

Without cutting the motor, he drops them on the other side of the wide canal in front of the Redentore. They practically have to jump, dodging the people waiting to go back. The man pays no attention to the passengers in the line, closes the gate on the empty motorboat, and speeds away.

The marble space in front of the church is awash: wind snarls the women's hair.

Inside, a priest points them to the sacristy. In glass bells, like physics experiments, wax heads, gristly with real-hair eyebrows, beards like upholstery stuffing, and glass eyes aimed heavenward, a vast array of saints with no explanation to say they are not real causes Ursula to gape. Hands, shin bones, bits of true crosses, grills, racks, the torturous devices of hagiographic life line lace-edged shelves.

"Not real," Minnie says.

"Not real, that painting," Ursula retorts. She gazes into the eyes of her saint, becoming to Minnie's vision almost weightless.

"You want to see others?" the priest asks, examining Ursula.

"The lechery of these people," Minnie thinks, reddening.

The priest opens a giant armoire, takes down monstrances, silver pyxes, glass tubes, some with nothing more than a hair in them, a single hair of someone, Minnie imagines, who has done no more than she, flown, fallen, been thrown down a flight of crowded stairs, spilled blood. Each relic has an elaborate verification signed by an ecclesiastical official, the paper heavy with red wax seals, darkened now by age to the color of blood.

In the stuffy sacristy, Minnie has trouble breathing. Her stitches pull as if her head were swelling. She goes outside where several people are still standing in line for the boat. Gradually they leave the queue. One man remains, reading a week-old Rome newspaper. She can tell it is old by a photograph on the cover of an attempted assassination of a Vatican secretary in a foundling home. She wonders why no boats are coming. A gondola, tacking, dodging high waves, poles toward them. The gondolier, a daring expression on his face, shouts something to the man. They call back and forth, the man getting so excited Minnie thinks he is going to throw himself into the water. The gondola stands offshore looking up and down the *fondamenta*. His uneasy balance in the high waves reminds her of something the doctor said. "You're carrying something downstairs? Fall? You have to decide! Between your possessions and your life! You have to let go!" A fall, she thinks, is like a stickup. Nature had its hoodlums just as man did.

"What did he say?" she asks the man.

"They're on strike," he says.

"The boats?" she asks, incredulous.

"They may settle it today? Next week?"

"Next week?"

An island, she thinks helplessly, only one bridge from it to another island, the Giudecca she has made fun of where there will be no place to stay, eat, for the money they have. She wishes she had the bills she spent on the picture.

"Why?" she asks.

"Their cheese isn't ripe," the man says. "Their wine's too warm! They need a reason? I think it's the storm."

She calls to the gondolier. He shifts in toward her. "How much?" she demands.

"For what?" he says.

She presses her lips together, furious.

He names an exorbitant fee.

"Across!" she says stamping her foot. "Not to Naples! That's robbery!"

The gondolier nods in amicable agreement. "They probably not strike long," he says placatingly. "When the wind dies? They eat their lunch?"

She watches him turn back across the water, his oilcloth sailor hat almost disappearing in the swells. I could swim, she thinks. She remembers reading they used to lay a bridge across the canal during Ascension so penitents could cross to pray. Ursula is right, she thinks. They need a new washing machine.

Inside the church, the other man has pushed three chairs together, made a tent of the old newspaper over his face. In a small room behind the altar Ursula is looking at an exhibition of prints entitled *Venezia come era*. She stares at Venice, "as it was," sea monsters bubbling up in the very water Minnie has been thinking about swimming in. Minnie considers the little prints, clean and fresh, neatly framed in *passe-partout*; they put her overblown, dirty, crazed, suggestive paintings to shame. She wants to confess to the priest her pictures represent her husband's taste, not her own, but he tries to charge her admission to the exhibition though he obviously has let Ursula in free.

Her young eyes spot details lost to Minnie, who keeps running out to see if the strike is ended.

The priest says, "Signora? You have to decide?"

"There's nobody here! What difference does it make?" she says.

"In or out!"

She hears rain on the lead roof.

"In," she says. "If we miss that boat . . ."

"What? Signora? What will you do?"

Cowed, she watches him walk around the pictures with Ursula pointing things out until he is very close to her and Minnie can almost see their breaths mingling, like figures marching in step. He shows her two painted forms embracing in a seventeenth-century window, the man wearing a Punchinello face, the woman's shift up exposing her buttocks. In the next window of the print, a maid, her finger to her nose, empties a slop bucket.

Minnie wanders around the pictures twice, torn between losing her admission fee and missing the boat. The evenness of the pictures bothers her. She tilts one. The priest rushes up and straightens it, wags his finger at her. The room begins to sweat, fogging the glasses of the prints. Perspiration creeps past Minnie's dress shields. She walks faster and faster in the circle, depressed by the neatness, the order. She knocks another picture crooked, not certain her action has been deliberate. The priest goes to the door and sounds an alarm.

"Ursie!" she cries. "Make him shut it off!"

A few minutes later, a policeman miraculously appears. His face seems familiar to Minnie. It comforts her. She thinks of the law being on her side. Ursula, her face shining, recognizes her *poliziotto* from the day of Minnie's accident.

Minnie wishes she had the feeling, knew, she was being followed, premonition a compensation in age for the lost beauty of youth, but, like the night six years ago when her husband's boat sank with him aboard, she perceived nothing. "I'm not psychic," she admits sorrowfully aloud.

The others do not hear her, the priest explaining in rapid fire that Minnie has been damaging works of art, an affront to the Church in Rome, the government of Italy, and Art in general. He exchanges hand signs, Minnie imagines, of deep-rooted obscenity with the policeman. They are in the nave of the church now, their voices rising to Palladio's vaults, the open door admitting sunlight which garnishes a small motor launch at the foot of the steps, the police department cipher blazed on the stern.

The policeman turns to Minnie and bows: "We go?"

The three of them pile into the boat, which peels away from the quay with the swift decisiveness of a building being demolished, slaps the waves, sprays water in their faces. Seeing Ursula snug against the policeman, Minnie feels deflated, wants to take credit for the rescue, the romance, but remembers her husband's promise to Ursula's mother, his betrayal. The view of the Dogana, the Piazzetta on her left, mocks her with its crowds of frivolity. She feels deserted by art, the past she has clung to. She does not open her mouth to protest when Ursula, by accident or design, lets her picture slide into the water. She hears the waiting passengers in front of San Giorgio cheer wildly as a *vaporetto* cleaves toward them, the end of the strike.

They get home late, drenched. The figs are mush. Minnie thinks Ursula sat on them. Instead of reprimanding her in front of her policeman, she thinks she will be sick. But Ursula is already in the bathroom. Minnie bangs on the door.

"I'm sick!" Ursula calls from inside. Minnie puts her ear to the door to verify the illness. Satisfied, she makes up her own bed for the girl, the little walnut *putti* on the headboard grinning. She lays out a robe for her: to make room for a chamber pot, drags a picture from under the bed into the living room. She stands on a stool and tries to tack the bull's head back on "The Rape of Europa" stretcher, refusing the policeman's offer of help.

"Don't forget to duck," she says, not sure to whom she is saying this. The young policeman sits primly, a proper suitor.

Ursula emerges from the bathroom, pulls him up from his chair to show him where she sleeps in the kitchen while Minnie goes into the toilet.

In the living room again, Ursula offers him a tiny glass of *grappa*. The lights dim, the aftermath of every storm in Chioggia, flicker, then go off. They sit in the dark room, the paintings shining like distant beacons in the rain, while the three of them drink the bitter aperitif. Ursula goes back into the bathroom: Minnie follows, tells her since she is sick to sleep in her room. Then she goes into the kitchen through the hall. Flat on the uncomfortable cot, exhausted, she thinks of the sleepless night ahead, of sleepless nights of the past. She hears the floor creak, imagines it is Titian. The voice is soft, calling a woman's name. Defensively Minnie tells herself it could almost be the cat's purr. Her throat congeals. She feels the warmth of presence, like a candle in the room, smells the policeman's beautiful hair Ursula has dried with one of *her* embroidered towels. The transition from air and presence to the kiss astonishes her. Lying back against her age, time itself, she wonders how he can realize his mistake so quickly, does not want to know, grasps at the thought it isn't a mistake. He rescued them *both*, she thinks. Her breath comes short, fast, then evenly, the promise and memories of sleepless nights fading into the sound of rain falling. Her eyes open and shut like water lapping against the landing stages. She is so tired. Tomorrow, the stitches come out. Awake, she tries for the sound of the front door closing after the young man, indicating his departure, the guarantee of Ursula's chastity; asleep, she cannot hear it.

The Glass of Milk

Annie Lee, hating her name and clutching a peanut butter and jelly sandwich, starts up the back stairs, her stairs. The front stairs have turned balusters, shiny brass carpet rods, but these steps are bare. Plain square sticks hold up the rail, which is circular, raised up from its base like a running sausage. The light bulb in these back stairs—for servants once—has been out from the time her parents bought the house when she was seven. Someone, not her, would have to get two ladders, one to prop up to the landing and another to lay across the well to stand on to reach the dangling socket. Annie Lee hopes no one will ever replace it.

She is depressed, alone in the house as usual. She tries to cheer herself with the prospect of calling herself AL at school where she is not popular, dressing like a boy, cap, corduroy pants, too-big sweaters, becoming a living dare to the people who don't pay any attention to her.

She knows she should've put the sandwich on a plate. Her mother forbids food upstairs anyway. She wonders where her mother is. Buying another outfit for her. She wishes—"to hell," she says out loud—she could buy her own clothes. Her only hope is in her brothers' hand-me-downs. "What do boys wear?" she thinks, licking peanut butter from her wrist. She suddenly thinks she should've brought some milk, goes back to the kitchen, pours herself a plastic glass (left over from her mother's cocktail party last week), and balancing the sandwich on top of the glass starts back up again.

Her right hand feels the rail. It has been sanded down, smoothed by years of use. She grips it lightly with her fingers. Its shape reminds her of seeing her brother, Paynter, naked in the bathroom Saturday.

She'd gone into his bathroom because it had a shower and hers didn't. She had stayed a long time, smoothing the soap over her body, touching her new breasts, reveling in the pleasure of being by herself and menstrual. She had just finished the

131

shower, had turned off the water and was letting it dry on her skin. The shower curtain was pulled across the stall when he came in. Annie Lee hadn't locked the bathroom door. She hadn't thought there was anybody in the house. Most of the time there wasn't. Her mother was always off buying something. Doctor Daddy was curing cancer. The housekeeper, Mamacita (a name the woman called herself to try to endear herself to the family), was fooling around in the garden or asleep from the effort of cooking breakfast. Paynter, naked, came into the bathroom. He leaned over the hand basin, unconscious of what she had heard so much about and never seen. It flopped on the ledge of the white enamel basin; she was astonished at its color, at its seeming to have a will of its own, at its potential embarrassment to its owner; where, she wondered, not daring to breathe, would he keep it when it wasn't being used?

She was terrified he'd see her; she reddened at the thought he might accuse her of spying. She couldn't stop watching, though. Wanted to. He attacked a pimple on his chin, leaning into the mirror of the medicine chest. From the rear, he looked almost like her except he had no hips and the bathing suit line around the back and under the armpits from a bra top was missing. His legs were covered with fuzz, but not much more than hers would be if she didn't shave. He kept pushing against the corner of the sink. The corner—it was an old-fashioned washbasin on a stand—was between his legs as he put his face close against the glass; she could see the mist of his breath, almost breathe it herself if she had been breathing. He wiped it away with his hands, wholly intent on his face. Slowly, he moved into the sink, pressing himself against the smooth white enamel, and then, as slowly, pulling away. She felt her heart slugging against her chest. The object, the strange tube of flesh—she knew the name, could say it if she were breathing— lay and seemed to swell, actually to grow, on the shelf of the hand basin. She was sweating. The shower stall had no vent: the moisture from the tiles closed in on her. She imagined the smooth cool of the enamel hand basin he felt pressing against his body. She envied his having this strange difference.

She liked Paynter, he seemed to like her. Seeing him naked this way made her feel something stronger for him. St. John, her other brother, St. John, "Saint" to rhyme with his twin, Paynt, though called John, barely tolerated her, went through her dresser drawers looking for something, anything, a rubber band, a safety pin, her panty hose to put on under his ski pants, and threw everything on the floor. She had no secrets from him. She didn't exist except as an annoyance for him, or as a source, someone to steal things from. But Paynt came by her room when she was crying. Gave her her first toke. Asked her sometimes to go with him downtown. John never let her go with him anyplace, wouldn't be seen at school with her. Most people didn't even know they were related. She felt for Paynt something, something, pleasure in being with him; she felt hopefulness from his being really nice to her that later, one day, somebody else might like her, too—someday—might feel something for her. She didn't dare say the word, like the word for the part of his body that was stiff and seemed strong though moments ago it had been limp as cloth, something? Love? "Love your brother," the graffiti said. Love. But something was wrong. As wrong as her being there in the first place, not breathing in the shower stall. It was wrong though nothing else she had ever felt, nothing, felt as good as the feeling of being with him, even of thinking about him; and had she been really like him and had that thing too, she would've shown it off to her friends at school, and used it and that would have made her popular, that would've proved once and for all she was the biggest dare, and she would've thanked her brother for that.

Now, going up the stairs in the dark, she sees him in her mind that day, the moment when his face pigged against the mirror, his eyes rolled back into his head, his butt pushing faster and faster into the washstand until he made the noise of an animal locked up in a pen trying to get out and a shower of something, she knew what that was, too, like melted ice cream splattered all over the bathroom floor. He stood there, trembling a moment. She thought he might be having a convulsion. He leaned back, completely lost in himself and a kind of splendor flushed his face. She thought he was beautiful. The tan, the white line where his bathing suit separated what the world saw from what she was seeing, the brief twitch, than the elegant looseness of all his muscles made her think she was seeing something that united her with all the other women of the world. It made her a woman, seeing. She knew at that moment he would discover her. That would wreck their friendship. But he didn't see her. He existed at that second only for himself. She thought even if he'd seen her he wouldn't have seen her.

She opens the door at the top of the stairs to the hall. She takes a sip of the milk. She walks down the hall to her room. The door is open. St. John has been in her room. He took her Coppertone, probably smeared himself with it and left the half-empty jar open on her bed where it turned over and in the heat is melting and staining the sheets. She picks it up and sets the milk and sandwich on the floor, by her bed. She takes a bite of the sandwich and lies down wondering why it doesn't bother her she is dripping peanut butter on the sheets the way her brother dripped suntan oil.

"Somebody else's mess," she says to the sandwich.

"What?" It is Paynter, standing in the doorway. He is wearing his underpants. Usually the three of them, her twin brothers and herself, do not go between each other's rooms that way.

"I brought you something," he says. "This is a tube but it's just as good as the jar." He hands her a tube of Coppertone. "I'm sorry Saint got in your stuff. He's just a natural drawer puller. Give me a bite?"

"No! Get your own!" she says, sorry the minute she's said it.

"Just a little," he says, coming close.

"No!" She smiles and tries to cram the sandwich in her mouth to keep it from him.

"Oh, no you don't," he says, trying to grab it from her hand. Some of the peanut butter falls on his arm. Without thinking beyond that it is hers, she licks it off just as he lunges for the sandwich. His body seems to her to give off extreme heat. His skin against hers makes her tingle. It is a kind of warmth that is like fire you want to touch. You don't draw back from it.

"Give!"

"No!" she says. "It's mine!"

"One bite," he says, chomping down on the sandwich at the other end.

His being there in his jockey shorts, his tumbling onto her bed, his mouth that close to hers, and the heat he is giving off scare her with pleasure she doesn't understand. She is wearing a halter, shorts.

"No!" she squeals. "Get up!" She pushes him off the bed. He lands on the floor, upsetting the glass of milk.

"Now look what you've done!" She tries to sound mad. He lies back on the bed, parallel to her. She is surprised at how quickly he gets back on her bed. A railroad track, his body next to hers. They could go on like this, never meeting but being together, she thinks. Permanently close. Their legs are straight, Annie Lee thinks, straight and pretty. Orange-brown from the summer.

He says, "You are thinking? If at all?"

"I'm thinking I have to clean up the spilt milk. You know what milk that's soured smells like on a carpet after a week?"

"Gardenias?"

"You guess everything!"

"You smell good," he says.

"Peanut butter. A favorite perfume."

"No, you do."

She wants to tell him he smells good. He doesn't exactly. A kind of salt, wet milkshake odor. Her heartbeat, she thinks, follows a pattern like rickrack along the bottom of her rib cage. She is afraid to talk. Somehow, without either moving, they are touching along their legs. The fringe of hair along his legs touches her, makes her twitch; he puts his hand very gently, almost timidly, under her neck and brings his mouth to her cheek very near her mouth and kisses her, a kiss that meets the skin of her face openmouthed, warm, soft; she thinks her mother must be standing in the door, threatening, promising punishment. She pulls away from him. He says, quietly, "You're a good girl, AL." His mouth stays on her cheek moving toward her ear with its message, riding, like a platform, just above the skin. She goes rigid, hates herself for sounding stiff and unnatural.

"I'll make you a sandwich."

"I don't want a sandwich," he says. His mouth is still there. The breath, the same breath she saw on the mirror in the bathroom that day, hangs in suspension between the lips it left and the ear it is aimed for. "Annie!" he says.

She can't speak. She moves her leg, she thinks of it as west; she has to get up and find a paper towel to clean up the milk. "I'll smell that. I have to get something." She feels she is in a glass box. She hits the glass wall that surrounds her and it paralyzes her every resolution to move.

"Annie," he says, his voice low as a call in the woods, some animal's cry. She rolls, her body almost unknown to her, a load of uncooperative bricks, not away from him—she convinces herself she meant to move away—right into him. He is rigid, his hand firmly behind her neck. She looks into his face with such a strong presumption of innocence that he smiles, unmoving, frozen almost but for the heat he gives off.

She has never looked anybody in the face before. She always glances in shyness, or defiance, away. The hours she has stared into the mirror wondering what she could do to change, what plastic surgery cost, wondering if someone, anyone, would ever like her, or look at her the way she was looking at herself, have failed to prepare her. Paynter's face is honest, straight. The features she has not liked in her own face strike her as beautiful in his. His eyes, green with light and dark flecks of what appears to her orange and brown from his sunburn, open up into an absence that seems to need her, want her. She feels the tips of her little breasts against the white cotton halter. The light in the room from the windows settles in the green, inflames the orange.

He keeps saying, "You are thinking?" She listens for the question mark, doesn't hear. His not touching her is much more painful than something she could feel with physical closeness or violence. She puts her leg backward, she thinks, as if she is marching away. She is staring so deep into his eyes she cannot blink. Her senses seem to be switched off at her main circuit box. Her nostrils open in a desperate attempt to catch the smell of peanut butter as her only reality, the smell of summer, of outside, of the room with her little bottles of perfume. But there is only the salt smell of his body. She can hear, she thinks, his breathing but she realizes it is her own. He is moving his lips, saying something. She thinks how wise, how much older he is, cleverer than she is, not to say anything, but to say, since she cannot fathom what he is actually saying, everything.

"Do you want to?" he might have been saying. But it could've been, "No, get up now." She hears him shouting in the distance though he is an inch away. "Annie Lee? Yoo hooo? Come to earth. Want to see what I bought you?" Her mother's voice, taking on a stolid meaningfulness, steps out of Paynter's mouth, the same march and direction her leg moved away from him with. "You want a sandwich?" The voice screeches through Paynter's mouth. The mouth is his, hers, St. John's, her mother's. Their voice. It runs up the back steps and crashes into the door. Annie Lee can hear it now, but she isn't moved by it. Every voice, teacher, father, mother, she has heard and not heeded stops now at the pine door, the rough, dark door that closes off her stairs from the white kitchen with the botanical prints on the walls, the needlepoint sampler that says "Bless This Mess," the rooms that have been done over and the ones that haven't. Nothing has been touched on the back stairs. They are hers. Her mother's voice tries to ascend: the door throws the voice back.

Annie lies still, scared at the noise her breath makes. Paynter looks at her as if the sound of her breath is striking him deaf. He gets up from her bed, grabs a towel from the bathroom doorknob, and wraps it around him. He snatches a necktie— his father's—an effort of Annie Lee's to look like a boy—and ties it around his sweating neck as their mother throws the door wide, then closes it a little.

She stands for an instant, the heritage of mothers suspecting their children heavy on her. Her nose breaks down the smells of the peanut butter sandwich, the glass of spilled milk, something else her brain hesitates over and lets go quickly.

Annie Lee stares up at her mother with a kind of respect Paynter's absurd costume has failed to destroy. She wonders if her mother saw her father the way she saw Paynter, whether she was able to appraise him from the privacy of a shower stall or whether she had to take him on faith. Out of that faith she was born or out of that knowledge. She hopes it was knowledge. That would mean they meant her. "What is that smell?" her mother asks.

With two older brothers, Annie Lee thinks, it is bound to have been knowledge. She begins to answer her mother.

Point of Conversion

Mrs. Clementson had had pregnant girls before. Father Sheehan sent them mainly, but they'd come from the Welfare, too. Even from what she still called the WACs. The girls came, swelled for their months, weeping copiously about the men who'd done them wrong, laid their egg, then painted their faces to go out and do it all over again. But they left. That was the point. They left. Verna hadn't. After Verna's baby was born, and Mrs. Clementson, or Clemmie as everybody called her— the social tongue never saw fit to title her—stood masked in the delivery room and saw a bungling nurse carry the baby out the wrong door for adoption so that Verna, alert, insistent on natural childbirth, the exercises, the breathing, saw the baby, saw her baby and Godknowswhoelse's baby, saw it was a boy baby, saw that she would never see him again, and in sobs stayed with Mrs. Clementson.

Clemmie was glad at first. In this garden that she as an ex-public-health nurse ran, where girls blew up and never grew up, Verna seemed to learn. Was hurt. Would do better. Clemmie was retired now. Sixty-five, on a pension, living in her grandmother's house, dead now, the grandmother and the house, a Victorian draft with a roof like a saltshaker. But rooms. Rooms gone to bed. So that was how Father Sheehan got her into this. And they paid her for it, too. They, the church, the county, the state, the government. "Did you know that?" she said to Mary Murphy, her oldest friend, her roommate, her sounding box. "Did you know that the government—you and I—pay for the girl to have her baby? Then give her six weeks of postnatal care? The WACs. Did you know that?"

Mrs. Murphy, oldest and dearest, yawned. She had become a crank. Was not retired. Completely taken up with her job at the Veterans' Hospital. Smoked. Wore her hair in a tumble.

When time finally shrank Verna, Clemmie got her a job at a friend's office. Typing out statements. The Madonna Shop. Bills. Orders. The shop sold greeting cards, penny pictures of vapid Jesuses made in Italy to women who stuck them in books and forgot about them. Verna was not a Catholic. And that was the wonder. After all, it was to Father Sheehan she talked in the months of agony when she wondered why the boy she loved wouldn't marry her and be happy with the child she was going to give him. "You wouldn't want to marry him if he doesn't love you now, would you?" Father asked the girl in the back room. Clemmie washed supper dishes, and wondered why he didn't close the door, though knowing that he could never forget—and how could she?—that she was a convert, hence some different sort of clay, clay that had to have it explained by open doors and commonplace chats over commonplace cups of coffee that there were no secrets in the church, no mysteries that she herself couldn't partake of. "I could tell you what they're like. Men. Use you like Kleenex, then toss you in the garbage." Her own experience was brief. Husband who drank. Divorce that didn't leak.

Verna went on weeping. But she wouldn't be baptized. Wouldn't. Went to mass with Clemmie, Sunday, twice a week, sometimes more. Sat there in the pew. Knelt. Recited. But wouldn't come in. "Why in heaven's name?" asked Mary Murphy. "She only talks to Father Sheehan. Thinks he's wonderful, goes with you fifty times a week to mass. Why?" She yawned. Verna said sometimes, "I know everybody thinks I'll get over this. But I won't. You don't know. I'll never, never get over it." Clemmie looked in a Blue Horse notebook she kept and read the names of fourteen girls she'd kept who had had illegitimate babies. "And you won't get over it," she thought. So Verna kept on with the greeting cards and penny pictures and helped out at the house which didn't make Clemmie mad, since she'd taken in two old ladies who couldn't stand a rest home, and whose two nieces said, "Will you take them, Clemmie?" and Clemmie, seeing the nieces' chops water in anticipation of the estate, smiled and said, "Yes. Two hundred apiece." Anyone else she would have done free. She liked to take care of people, wait on them. "You should've been a waitress," Mary Murphy said.

"I was," Clemmie came back. "A waitress with bed pans and enemas and specimens. A white-winged waitress."

"Talk yourself into paradise," cranked Mrs. Murphy.

Verna was young. Never answered back. Ran errands. To the grocery. To the parish hall. To wherever in the world Clemmie wanted her to go. Lickety-split. Clemmie was deep into the Catholic family parish life. Nuns from Sacred Heart School came to supper. She had, almost, a brogue, from Father Sheehan, from Mrs. Murphy, from the brothers, the sisters, the fathers. An occasional Monsignor. People even said—people who knew her when she was Scotch, when she was Presbyterian, when her father played the pipe organ at the First Presbyterian Church and her mother taught Sunday School, people who knew her before the conversion—the conversion of St. Clemmie, Mrs. Murphy called it, and after half a bottle of sherry drew it on the tablecloth; Clemmie struck by light, Clemmie on her knees, stigmata spiking her hands, her tennis-shoed feet, Father Sheehan holding the reins of her bike—people, at parties or any other place where Clemmie, on her bike, in her Nash Metropolitan, went, said, "Now, look at her. If she isn't the epitome of Irish Catholic potato famine, the *epitome*." And Clemmie didn't mind because her potato-famine Irish friends were jolly and common-to-the-core and who, she herself included, wasn't? And being ostracized, Greek for pottery shard, said Mary who knew everything unimportant—"Broken pieces of pottery and you wrote the name of some crook politico on it and if he got enough—out, and I could think of a few, the mayor included, I'd like to break pottery on"—being ostracized from the non-Irish didn't mean anything but being taken in by the Irish. Besides it was 19——? and nobody was anybody but out of the melting pot. "Everybody else her age has a pot. Except her. She's always pedaling off her pot on her bike. Other ladies peddle insurance but fair Clemmie pedals pot."

(Mrs. Murphy on the subject.) And Verna didn't feel so alone if someone else was ostracized. Verna. A mother without a mother's child. But wouldn't she come in? If the haves threw you out, shouldn't you go in with the have-nots? Anyway, not all of them were so have-not. The O'Shaughnessys owned a liquor store—a chain of them and if the haves didn't think that made mon, and fun . . . Mrs. O'What's-her-name shot Mr. O'What's-his-name's lover—and him with eight children . . . as the lover descended the bus at the corner of Amiens and Roule Street in full view of Tabby O'Something else who clerked in Mr. O's booze store number 6, but who refused to testify at the trial, saying he was under the counter when it happened though as everybody who'd ever had so much as a sip of Italian Swiss Colony knew, store number 6 was a glass box with no counter to speak of and inside you could see everything that took place in this world including the mating of an insect which Tabby had also noticed, Mr. O' and his lady love having rented a room in the building opposite number 6. And every Christmas, Easter, and All Saints' Day, having been acquitted, Mr. O' sent his lawyer, and Tabby, a case of Dewar's scotch and if that wasn't mon and fun, what was?

Why Verna wouldn't come in, into that cozy, chatty, warm-your-bones-by-the-fire-with-a-little-whiskey Irish life, God only knew. But she wouldn't.

She was from a little town in east Tennessee, "a teeny eenie iny town" of 150 with a high school that graduated two. (Verna was voted, she said, most likely, the other girl most beautiful.) Well, naturally, she was suspicious, but not old enough to have prejudices, especially old prejudices. Ate her breakfast eggs any kind of way.

Thursday, Clemmie pedaled to the Madonna Shop. Verna was out to lunch and her boss, Clemmie's old friend, said, "I'm going. Closing up shop and going. Pilgrimage. The holy land or Rome. Can't decide. Or maybe even Dublin." This with a wink and a slap on the rear, a conscious Irish manner which all of a sudden Clemmie found not quite so cute as she had pictured it to Verna who was on the outside looking in.

Verna was out of a job. It was all right when she was working and bringing in something for her room and board and going out on errands and helping around the house that really needed help. Now she wasn't part of the hive—the economic part—she'd never picked up with the social part. "Maybe I use her," thought Clemmie. "Maybe she uses me. The uses of uses. Anyway, she ought to have something, something to do."

Verna's unemployed status made her sulk, made her consider any employment—going to the grocery store, the parish—a drudgery. Clemmie sent her to the greengrocer and Verna banged the cabbage and squash down on the kitchen table with the change. "Here, here, this won't do," Clemmie schoolteachered. And Verna female-logicked right back, "Won't do? Well, count the change. It's all there. Look at the ticket if you think I took any of your money," and stormed out of the room.

Thursday a week, Clemmie heard the front door slam. Tears—she heard tears—Verna going through the living room, the parlor, the dining room, then into her own room. Another slam. More tears. Clemmie went to the front door. "Now why wouldn't she go straight down the hall to her room instead of zigzagging through every chamber in this heavenly mansion?" Following Verna's steps—her tears, she thought, but actually it was raining—she found a letter moiréed with the water from Verna's eyes or the sky's—she picked it up and read—none of her business but after all she had examined penises in the public health service.

My dearest darling V. My thoughts—and my prayers have been with you this last month. I praid your baby (your baby! bracketed Clemmie) was safely delivered. You would have been a wonderful and devoted mother. (You.) Since leaving you and the army, I have tried to build a new life for myself. Dad is happy with the progress I am making in college and thinks I can easily assume a position in his business when I graduate. But I am not kidding myself. I know it will be hard work. The whole thing has been very painful for me. (Painful. Oh I wish men could lay eggs.) But I believe everything has worked out for the better. Dad has given me a new car and this afternoon I have been out driving around with a friend. We stopped by a hillside and just walked around for hours, doing nothing, just staring off into space. Perhaps you and I can go for a ride some-day. Seattle is a long way for you to come, though, but who knows?

May the Lord help you as he has helped me. I know you will soon forget me and if sometime in the far distant future our paths should cross, you would say, Who was that? I don't remember. But I will never forget.

Yours very truly,

R. B. H., Jr.

When Mary Murphy came home from work, Clemmie said, "Verna is in her room crying."

"Well, I'll be in mine crying if I don't get these shoes off."

"Well, what's wrong with you?"

"Cement."

At supper, her feet reposing in red bunny slippers, Mrs. Murphy read the letter. Verna would not come out of her room. The old ladies—two hundred dollars—ate in theirs. "Why would she cry over that?"

"I can't guess," Clemmie said. Sarcasm.

"Well, I'll tell you one thing. Every country has its type. In La Belle it's the aging French *bébé*, England's got the moustache, and we have the Dear John."

"Her name's Verna."

"Don't smart it. Just pour the sherry," Mary said. "All right." Verna wept for R. B. H., Jr., her job, her baby. "Well, can you get her another job?" Clemmie asked. "Yes, if we don't get flooded out of the front door."

The next day, Mary Murphy paddled down the hall to the source of Verna's tears and told the girl she had a job for her— temporary replacement in a doctor's office. Verna . stopped weeping long enough to go to work. A week went by and she liked it. Breezed in and out. Clemmie mopped up the hall.

Before, Verna had walked to work. Or ridden Clemmie's bike. The Madonna Shop was only four blocks away. Now she had to drive. Clemmie lent her the Nash. Mary: "Is she careful?" Clemmie: "Is she timely? I've got to go to mass five minutes before she gets back."

A month she was on time. Then she wasn't. Clemmie, in hat and coat, temporally and spiritually prepared for the mass, was in flame. "Where have you been? Where! You know I'm late to mass already when you get here. Now it's too late, and here I am lending you my car."

"That car!" Verna said.

"Well you can walk tomorrow, then." Clemmie took off her hat and coat, her armor of light. Verna went to her room. Clemmie put on her apron and started peeling potatoes. "Verna!" she called. "You get in here and peel these!" Verna came out and peeled them, her large clumsy fingers leaving in the eyes and gouging out most everything else.

Next day she walked to work, came home with two friends, two pregnant friends. "This is Louanne and Becky. They were in the army with me. Now the same thing's happened to them." She giggled. They went to Verna's room. Shut the door. Giggles. Clouds of smoke.

When Mary got there, they came out and were introduced. They were leaving anyway. They giggled. Rested their arms on their stomachs. "What's so funny? You think a pin'll make that go down?" They giggled harder, went out the front door, up the street, laughing to cry.

At 8:15, Mrs. Tonley, the regular nurse in the office where Verna worked, called. Mary knew her. They were chummy.

"I've asked her," Mrs. Tonley said. "She won't give me an answer. August is my vacation. I can't leave the doctor with nobody. I want to know if Verna's going to stay. Or what."

"We thought she loved the job."

"I think she does. I just want to know about August."

In the doctor's office next day Mrs. Tonley said to Verna, "What I want to know is are you going to be here August? Or aren't you? All of it."

"See, I really do like it here. You and Dr. Blake are real good to me. I put in for this government job at the fort. Teaching. That's what I did in the army. I don't know if I'll get it. Then you know I get the GI bill. But I'm saving that."

"That's fine. Are you going to be here August? Else I've got to get somebody who will."

"Well, see, teaching—like I was doing in the army—it's all I really know how to do. I know what to teach them."

"I bet you do," said Mrs. Tonley, and the doctor rang. Some patient couldn't get back into her panty hose. Geriatrics.

Next day, Mrs. Tonley said, "Which, Verna? Now. Decide."

"Oh, Mrs. Tonley . . . If they accept my application at the fort I'd have to go right out. They have a lot of girls in line for the job . . ."

"Which, Verna? Now!"

"If they don't take me out there, I won't have a job."

"Verna, I want somebody here for August."

"I don't know."

Mrs. Tonley called Mary that night. "Tell her not to come in tomorrow. I got somebody else. I never saw anything like that girl. Wouldn't say."

"Don't blame me. She's none of mine. It's Clemmie brings home the strays around here."

"How is Clemmie, anyway?"

"She's all right. This'll give her something to do. Finding Verna a job."

"Something else."

When informed, Verna cried. Clemmie said, "Dear God," rising to the occasion by breaking out in hives. She couldn't lie on her bed. Couldn't wear clothes. Wouldn't give in. "I've got something better to do." In a hospital gown—all she could wear—hives and all, her hands pinching the flaps together over her naked behind, Clemmie went out to the hospital. "Don't you have some course out here in Practical Nursing?"

"Yes, ma'am. But you're too old."

"Well now, sonny, how old do you have to be?"

"Eighteen and a high school graduate. September fifth."

"Well, she's that."

On the spot, hives stinging like so many wasps, Clemmie enrolled Verna, at least as far as she could, she not having Verna's thumb prints, birth certificate, high school diploma, and a spare notary public.

Verna said no, she wouldn't go, wouldn't use her GI Bill, wouldn't. Said Clemmie could go herself if she wanted to go so bad. But, September fifth, she got her history together, got it notarized publicly, and went. Two weeks later, a boy brought her home. She was wearing a starched uniform, pink and white stripes. Smiling. "You look fairly pretty," Mary Murphy said to Verna.

The boy turned out to be a male nurse. Clemmie disapproved. "He hasn't got bat brains. And he's three years younger than she is."

"Oh, what do you know about love?" snided Mary.

Clemmie had given Verna back the car. Verna was later and later. Clemmie gave up mass. Sundays Verna worked part time in a nursing home. With him.

"She could do that around here," Mary said.

"I'm worried," Clemmie said.

"What you need is some more pg girls. To distract you . . . What's the moon doing tonight?"

"Gibbous waning."

"Nothing there."

One afternoon, Clemmie and Verna were out shopping. They rode by the First Baptist Church, biggest church in town. "That's where I'm going to be married."

"It's a lovely church," Clemmie said vaguely, wistfully. Vague because she couldn't think what Verna meant, or if she meant anything; wistful, because her own church took up two hundred dollars in the collection every other Sunday while this Goliath raked in a national debt.

He came to supper that night. During dessert—floating island—Verna said to him, him who never identified himself on the phone, said "Is Verna there?"—nothing else, ran through amber lights—him, seventeen and a male nurse—"Tell her." As easily as asking for more dessert—which he did—he told them.

Clemmie gritted her teeth: "I'm not going to break out in hives. Not." After he left, she went to Verna's room. "Is that what you want? Really want?"

"We love each other," Verna said.

"You've been through one junkbunk already. This probably won't be any better, will it?"

"This is going to make everything in my life all right. Everything I went through. We're going to have our own apartment, our own job, our own friends, our own baby, our own *car.*"

Clemmie went with her to the First Baptist where the preacher said it was fifty dollars for nonmembers to be married in his church which squelched that. And to the Key Wholesalers where they bought dishes and stainless steel, and sheets—what else does a man need to live by? Clemmie tried to remember.

Verna found another Baptist Church—it was called either the Third Baptist Church or the Fourth Baptist Church. Mrs. Murphy didn't bother to say, "What about Father Sheehan?" Verna and her boy wondered whether to wait till their year course was up. Clemmie said, "Yes. Do. You'd better." They decided not to.

"What is it?" Clemmie demanded of Mary Murphy. "What

don't we do right? I tried. I did for her . . . she can't deny that. Her parents wouldn't let her in the house. I let her. Maybe it's the generation gap."

"Generation gap? I should hope so. One of those 'youths' tries to get familiar with me, I'll break its . . ."

"No, I meant, maybe we can't talk to them."

"It's them can't talk to us. Mouths all stuffed up with bubble gum."

"Oh, Mary. Sometimes you're a comfort," Clemmie changed gear to a snicker, "and sometimes you're not."

"Has she told him?" Mary asked.

"What?"

"About the baby, the po'lil unwanted baby. 'It was just a little baby, your honor.'"

"Oh, dear God, Mary. It's not so funny. No. She hasn't told him."

"Well, don't you think she oughter?"

"She says he won't marry her if he knows."

"Won't he find out? On the wedding night?"

"She's going to a gynecologist."

"A gynecologist!"

"Yes, she says he can make her like she was before . . . Like a virgin."

"You get the name of that doctor."

When the male nurse kissed Verna good night in the hall, Clemmie, sitting up late with the Annals of Good St. Anne de Beaupré, saw them, thought, "What a pretty thing. Their kiss. Teeth hidden . . . Muted lips. Breathless wonder." He left her, lips first, last, the hands. As he left, Verna said, curiously, Clemmie thought, "Immersion?" "Total immersion," he said. Clemmie imagined. "Love. Totally immersed in love."

It was baptism they were speaking of, though. The following morning Reverend Reold called. "We are happy to have a new soul." "Who wouldn't be, brother?" thought Clemmie, fundamentalist emerging. "Happy with a new soul for our body, the church. Please tell the applicant to bring a large towel and a change of dry underwear."

"She wouldn't bring wet, now would she," said Clemmie, the receiver safely down, Mary's personality drenching her.

Clemmie got it all together and at six she and Mary stood behind the altar in the Fourth Baptist Church and watched Verna in a white robe walk down into the water. Then in the robing room they dried her and saw her without makeup, naked, saw how plain she was, how young, how forlorn.

The next day they were married. Clemmie and Mary stood on the steps of the church, the prefabricated church, stark and new ("Thank God for all our papier-mâché," confided Mary, hatted and respectable for the occasion), as Verna and her male nurse dashed for the Nash in a thin shower of rice given up by the two pregnant friends and Clemmie and Mary as far as their bursitised arms allowed. Clemmie thought of them driving—that was her wedding present, the car—driving, driving God knows where, God knows to what motel, driving, the insects, drawn by the lights, splattering against the windshield, and she felt a terrible sense of failure, terrible.

Other Iowa Short Fiction Award and John Simmons Short Fiction Award Winners

1988
The Long White, Sharon Dilworth
Judge: Robert Stone

1988
The Venus Tree, Michael Pritchett
Judge: Robert Stone

1987
Fruit of the Month, Abby Frucht
Judge: Alison Lurie

1987
Star Game, Lucia Nevai
Judge: Alison Lurie

1986
Eminent Domain, Dan O'Brien
Judge: Iowa Writers' Workshop

1986
Resurrectionists, Russell Working
Judge: Tobias Wolff

1985
Dancing in the Movies,
Robert Boswell
Judge: Tim O'Brien

1984
Old Wives' Tales, Susan M. Dodd
Judge: Frederick Busch

1983
Heart Failure, Ivy Goodman
Judge: Alice Adams

1982
Shiny Objects, Dianne Benedict
Judge: Raymond Carver

1981
The Phototropic Woman,
Annabel Thomas
Judge: Doris Grumbach

1980
Impossible Appetites, James Fetler
Judge: Francine du Plessix Gray

1979
Fly Away Home, Mary Hedin
Judge: John Gardner

1978
A Nest of Hooks, Lon Otto
Judge: Stanley Elkin

1977
The Women in the Mirror, Pat Carr
Judge: Leonard Michaels

1976
The Black Velvet Girl, C. E. Poverman
Judge: Donald Barthelme

1975
*Harry Belten and the
Mendelssohn Violin Concerto*,
Barry Targan
Judge: George P. Garrett

1974
*After the First Death There Is
No Other*, Natalie L. M. Petesch
Judge: William H. Gass

1973
The Itinerary of Beggars,
H. E. Francis
Judge: John Hawkes

1972
The Burning and Other Stories,
Jack Cady
Judge: Joyce Carol Oates

1971
Old Morals, Small Continents,
Darker Times, Philip F. O'Connor
Judge: George P. Elliott

1970
The Beach Umbrella, Cyrus Colter
Judges: Vance Bourjaily
and Kurt Vonnegut, Jr.